Hellbound

Angel

By Nikki Avila

Hellbound Angel

Published by Paradisiac Publishing
http://www.paradisiacpublishing.com

You can follow the author on Instagram @nikki.avila

Cover Art by Jasmine Ford – Art_By_Medusa@yahoo.com

ISBN-13: 978-0692853979

Too all those we lost too soon.

I don't think I'll ever stop

missing you.

Acknowledgements

First and foremost, I'd like to thank Lauren Wood and everyone at Paradisiac Publishing for giving my "world" a chance. Without your belief, I'd still be merrily typing away and hoping one day this book would end up on bookshelves everywhere. Jasmine Ford and Michael Leon, you made my thoughts into something more beautiful than I could've imagined. Covers draw people in and I'm sure this one will. Thank you for the time you spent drawing and redrawing as my mind took different directions. Josh Hancock, simply put, thank you for your time. As my English teacher, I knew I'd hit the jackpot. Somehow though, you're an even better person. Taking the time to read my entire novel and mark not only the mistakes but the small successes as well, is something I can never fully thank you for. That you too are an author who is very busy writing his own incredible tales, makes the time commitment that much more difficult and meaningful.

Mom and Dad. What to say? I could thank you for a thousand and one little things you've done that helped make this all possible. But it boils down to this: you believed in me. Whether that showed itself through letting me get on our household's one computer for hours on end or allowing me to talk your ear off about plans I had for this book and the next and the next. Truly, I couldn't have come this far without you. And I still need you. Always.

I've always believed the world to be black and white. You're born, you live, and you die. There is no Heaven or Hell. No angels and no demons. The monsters you imagined as a child were just that, imaginations.

I couldn't have been more wrong...

Prologue: year 2006

"She'll find her." Layna whispers, afraid to even utter her mother's name.

Alexander draws his wife close with his free arm. The other snuggled protectively around their precious baby. Even at a year she's so incredibly tiny, hardly twenty pounds, but strong too. Like her mother's her blue eyes brim with determination. Nothing can stop those two. Except for maybe Lilith.

"I won't let that happen," He soothes. On the inside, he's as desperate and as unsure as Layna. If he wasn't they wouldn't be doing this. But they'd never had to deal with this before. Never thought she'd come after their little angel. Didn't think she'd buy into the prophecy. But clearly that was a foolish hope and something needed to be done. This was that something.

"We'll have to change her name, both of them. Her birth date. She'll never know us." Layna babbles, tears dripping down her face.

"Sweetie, no. She'll know us. When the time is right," he says as he wipes away the traces of her anguish. "She keeps her name, you love your name don't you Leila," he effortlessly switches to baby talk, donning yet another mask for the innocent child.

She giggles, the sound jarring in an otherwise grief riddled room, and plants a wet kiss on her father's nose. Clueless.

"We'll change her birthday," Alexander agrees, "make it something in January and a year later. Her new parents," he nearly chokes on the word. This is his daughter. His. Right down to the shape of her perfect little nose. But they were doing this for her, he reminds himself. Because they love her, "will change her last name. She'll be safe."

"Safe." His wife repeats it like a prayer, something she'd never been known to do. Her mother would laugh at the irony.

I was drowning myself,

using the bottle to forget

the world.

Each one of the vile names

I'd been called became the pills

I was popping like candy.

The past curled its way around

my neck, a noose.

But I kicked the chair.

Damn if I didn't bring the

blow dryer in the tub with me.

Willing it to shock me back to life,

to the truth –

I was killer and victim

and God if it didn't have to stop.

Chapter 1

"Leeiii-llllaaaaa!" Annabelle's horror film worthy scream sets my blood on fire. If I can't see her, I can't help her. And thanks to the beautiful renovations of smoke and debris to downtown San Jose, I definitely can't see her.

"Annabelle, you okay?" Of course, when it mattered most I could think of nothing else to say and on top of that I was slowly starting to panic. The unfamiliar emotion was crawling down my throat and stealing the breath straight from my lungs. I was hyperventilating. Logically I knew that but with each second that passed with no answer from Annabelle it made me all the more helpless to stop it.

Careless of all the creepy crawlers that were bound to be around at this time of night, I start screaming for her, "Annabelle, please answer me! Annabelle!" *Stop!* I just needed to calm down and focus on my surroundings. Since I couldn't see much at all I decide to use my other senses. I could smell sulfur; a demon, and I could smell something coppery, which had to be blood. Annabelle's blood. Now if I could calm down and listen maybe, just maybe I could figure out which one of Hell's residents was messing with my sister. *Thwarp-Thwarp-Thwarp*. I could just barely make out the sound of broken wings laboring in the sky above me. It told me all I needed to know though -- I was dealing with an incubus. Nasty creatures for sure with their dangerous barbed tails, sharp claws, and such human like qualities but if I could de-wing the bastard I could kill it.

Problem one: thanks to the smoke I couldn't see the damn thing. Problem two: I was dangerously exposed. Problem three: and the worst by far, other than the oversized hunting knifes I usually tucked into each one of my gorgeous, worn, steel-toed black combat boots I was defenseless. Stupid me I left my crossbow with my bike ten-feet from here in my mad dash to Annabelle. That left me with one option; angering the poor lust demon down here. Great.

"Incubus, why don't you come out and play?" I was unconsciously circling now and watching the sky uneasily. "I swear all I want to do is kill you mercilessly!" my voice is in sing-song mode now. I don't even have to try. I've done this hundreds of times with all species of demons. "What are you a coward? Can't face one defenseless girl? Coward, coward, cow-"

"Aaaahhhhh!" damn bastard tore up my left arm before I got a chance to defend myself. He was a coward, a now tail-less coward. "That's right I got you too!" crippled as I am I should keep my mouth shut but I never do. Its shriek of rage fills the night sky as it doubles back and drops to the floor in front of me. The thing is truly ugly with features both demonic and human at the same time. Almost spellbinding. This I realize too late, like always, is the intent. Fire explodes on my face as the three wicked sharp talons on its right-hand slice into my cheek. Hesitantly, I touch the wound. The sticky feeling of already coagulating blood meets my fingers. It stings but I'll be okay.

Just in time I notice the incubus's hasty escape. Coward. Quickly and without so much as a second thought, I send one of my hunting knifes flying towards the incubi. It slides effortlessly into its chest stopping it in midflight. The sickening thud of body hitting concrete is the only thing that tells me the incubi hits ground. I stalk towards the sound ready to finish this so I can get to Annabelle. When I get to where the incubus has landed it is already up on its feet and limping away. I grab my second hunting knife and slice easily through the incubus's neck. Blood splatters across my face and chest as its body falls limp to its knees and then onto the ground, the head rolling away unceremoniously. I drop my knife and run towards Annabelle's unconscious body. A quick scan of the area shows that she is clearly alive, though she wouldn't be if she hadn't landed on some homeless person's discarded mattress, but fatally injured. The incubus's tail impaled her upper thigh, puncturing her femoral artery. She's hemorrhaging out. Panic threatens to take over my body but I push it down and tear off my shirt. Trying, unsuccessfully, not to think of the person I am treating here I use my shirt to put pressure on the wound. If I don't get the bleeding to stop and some help she'll be gone in minutes. Possibly seconds. I reach into my front pocket trying desperately to get a good grip on my phone knowing full well that every second could cost Annabelle her life. It takes a few tries with blood slick hands, but I manage. Meeting success in my first endeavor I try for the second: calling for help. Rudy thankfully answers on the first ring. "What's up?"

The sound of his voice breaks any self-control I still contain. "It's Annabelle. There was an incubus. And she fell. Her bike's totaled. And blood. Rudy, there's so much blood."

"Okay. Put pressure on the wound. Where are you?" how he understands me through the sobs now tearing out of my chest I don't know but I am thankful I don't have to repeat myself.

"Two blocks south of the front entrance."

"I'll be there in three."

My hands refuse to hold my phone any longer. It slides through crimson fingers and drops to the ground. Three minutes is too long. Annabelle will not make it three minutes. She is unconscious and bleeding. And dammit she could not die. She's all I have.

"Annabelle, you listen to me. You are not going to die. You can't. If you died I'd-" there was no answer to what I'd do. I had no idea. I'd never thought there would ever be a world where Annabelle wasn't here. It was impossible. Knowing there's nothing else I can do but keep pressure on the wound and hope for a miracle, I allow myself to be weak. I cry until Rudy arrives.

I hear boots hitting gravel and foolishly assume it's Rudy. Arms snake around my waist and yank me off the ground. I ignore my attacker's hushed attempts to calm me and his whispered *"it's okay, I'm a friend"* and start kicking and screaming, hoping that whoever grabbed me is afraid of the hellions I am probably waking up. He isn't. My attacker slaps his hand over my mouth and continues to drag me backwards. I fight with everything I have in me but I am out of weapons and my attacker has to be at least twice my weight and a good foot taller than me. So, I resort to fighting dirty: I aim a kick to his groin and bite the hand clamped over my mouth.

He grunts and buckles over. I'm not stupid though, he isn't anywhere close to down and out and I can't count on Rudy to save the day. My attacker has probably already gotten to him, a problem I'll deal with later. Right now, I need to focus on getting to Annabelle's unconscious form. If she did as I told her there would be a switchblade tucked into the waistband of her jeans. I only have to get to her.

I have to be at least five feet away when a hand lands heavily on my shoulder. Not waiting to be dragged away again I throw a right cross to his jaw. Crimson liquid pours instantly from his newly split lip and again the coppery smell of blood permeates the air, but I don't stop there. My left fist flies into his abdomen and he doubles over for the second time. I am squaring up for another round when Rudy's voice freezes me.

"Leila, stop! He's a friend!"

Friend? He has to be kidding me! "Some friend. He attacked me!" My tone is clearly indignant.

Ears hear what eyes are blind to: his exasperated sigh. "We don't have time for this Leila. Come help me get Annabelle settled in the truck. And Ezekiel if Leila didn't do too bad a number on you throw the bikes in the back."

My indignation sobers instantly at the mention of Annabelle. I rush over to where she still lay. Doing my best to ignore my once white t-shirt turned red with blood I grab Annabelle underneath her arms.

"Lead the way." I say.

The drive isn't more than five minutes, but it feels like a million years. Each second that passes is a year and every minute a thousand. Time is against us. Her heart has steadily been pumping out her life for the last ten minutes. No one can survive that. The wound is mortal.

By the time we get home I am numb and no longer any help. I have put up my wall, knowing fully that she has lost too much blood to survive. Wall intact, I shuffle out of the car and into our makeshift home. Without so much as a glance to anyone I pass, I head towards our filing cabinet turned liquor cabinet. Yes, I'm underage, but in the end of the world it doesn't matter, so I grab a bottle of vodka and head to the community bathroom to be alone.

I step into one of the many tiny showers and drop to the floor. Once under the spray of hot water, fully clothed but for my boots, I let my wall crumble. Every moment I had with her flashes before my tear blurred eyes. The first time I met her she was six and I was eight. From that moment on we were inseparable. I would know they had tried to separate us once.

The Child Protective Workers told us we were far too much trouble together. They hadn't seen anything yct. When they came to take Annabelle away they gave me a few moments alone with her to say our goodbyes. Walking into what had once been our room, I held back the sadness and instead let what I saw strengthen my resolve. Belle had tears steadily streaming down her face as she sobbed. When her eyes landed on me she threw herself into my arms. If she continued to cry I knew I would break down too. Determination clear on my face I retracted myself from her death grip and told her she needed to stop crying. The effort was visible, but she stopped immediately. I could still hear her choking down sobs; that I could deal with.

In a voice full of way too much wisdom for my eight years, I whispered, "You will not eat, you will not drink anything if you ever want to see me again."

"But Leila what if I get hungry?" At six years old that would be all she thought about.

Backtracking I asked her the only question that mattered: "Do you want to see me again?"

"Yes, you're my sister!" came her prompt reply. By blood we were no more related than a cat and a dog, but we were sisters bonded through turmoil.

Knock. Knock.

That would be CPS telling us it was time to go. I needed to hurry.

"Then Annabelle don't eat or drink. When they ask why, 'cause they will, tell them you won't eat anything until you get to be with me again." The words came out in a rush, but when understanding lit up her face I knew we would see each other again soon. "Belle I love you, I'll see you by dinner." A quick kiss on her wheat colored hair and I left the room.

"What's for dinner?" Her response made me proud and I couldn't keep a satisfied grin off my face as I walked by the CPS worker.

That was a moment I would never forget. It was in that moment I vowed to protect one of the three people who ever stuck by my side. I promised myself Annabelle would never hurt again.

I failed.

When I came to, the first things I notice are the color of the water –pink-- and a familiar looking face staring at me. Half drunk and half naked don't work so well when confronted by the gorgeous guy you punched in the face. Oops! Having no clue what to say I go for humor.

"You have a little something right there," I slur as I point to his split lip.

The chuckle he lets out is contagious and I can't help but laugh with him. Even when he stops it takes me a second. The vodka has officially taken over my brain.

In his cute accent I can't quite place, he points to me and says, "You're missing a little something right there." He is talking about my shirt, the one I used to try and stop Annabelle's bleeding. It hadn't worked. Deciding it was better to stay away from those thoughts for now I focus my attention on the delicious man in front of me.

"I'm sorry, does indecent exposure bother you?" I ask as innocently as I can muster.

His reply is quick and slightly rough. "Not on you it doesn't."

Girlish laughter escapes before I can stop it. Vodka. "Well, good, I don't wanna wait for Rudy to come help me get out of these soaked clothes."

The change that comes over him is sudden and sobering. "Rudy's seen you naked." He doesn't phrase it as a question, but I feel like I need to explain for Rudy's sake. The way this guy looks right now, he is ready to tear someone's head off. Which is odd.

"Not sexually or anything, but we get injuries that need treating. Clothing gets in the way."

"Injuries?" This change is just as sudden as the first, but this one makes my heart skip a beat. His face softens with worry as he searches my body for injuries. I see the instant he notices the scar on my hip. His touch is feather light as he traces its outline.

"How?" That one word is filled with so much sorrow and guilt. I don't know why or even understand why he feels like that, but I want so badly to make him laugh again. And that in itself raises some red flags for me. How can I care for someone I don't know?

Nonchalantly, I tell him an edited version of the story; "Pack of nasty hellhounds cornered me. I took out three in the first couple of minutes, but the remaining four were smarter than the first. One of them went for the right side of my hip," I motion to my scar, "while the others distracted me and lunged for my left ankle. The pain was excruciating, but I managed to decapitate them all." Did I though? Who knew? One moment I was up and adding yet another couple of scars to my body and the next thing I could remember was waking up to find that all the hellhounds had vanished, leaving behind nothing but massive puddles of blood. Someone had killed them, but I wasn't so sure it was me. I try to not to think about it too much though. Even now recalling the way their double sets of razor sharp teeth pierced into my flesh and muscle sends a shiver through my body. How deathly afraid I was to move, afraid that if I did flesh and muscle would tear right off my bone.

I make the idiotic mistake of revealing I had received two wounds in my first encounter with a pack of hellhounds. When Ezekiel doesn't immediately spot the wound he gently, as if the wound is fresh, pushes up the bottom of my jeans. Just as before when he catches sight of the scar a mixture of sorrow and guilt flashes across his face. It is only there for a brief moment, but it is there long enough for me to notice the change. I don't understand why at all though. It doesn't make any sense. The question needles me, becoming a nagging thought I can't rid myself of.

Yeah, these scars look bad, worse than others the way they clearly resemble the jaw of a dog of some sorts, but with my torso exposed as it is there are a million other little scars to see. Why is he stuck on these ones? Why is he stuck on anything at all? He doesn't know me and he certainly shouldn't feel guilty.

"Where was Annabelle?" His voice is barely above a whisper. Probably because he fears I'll take the question the wrong way. Take it like if she had been there I wouldn't have gotten hurt. His fear has merit.

I tamper down the anger at his mention of Annabelle and the suspicion at his caring at all and answer his question anyway. "She was in the truck." I reframe from explaining that she had only been fourteen, which is much too young to be any kind of help and that she would've caused more trouble on the ground with me.

He makes no comment and instead proceeds to ask yet another question. "What happened after?"

"Don't know. I had passed out and woke up to Rudy and Cara Marie treating my wounds." I try to keep my answers short and to the point. Despite his charming good looks something about this guy bothers me. He is asking way too many questions for comfort and I don't like the way he is looking at me. All are clear signs that I have sobered up and need to get back to my room and away from him.

I put my palms flat on the shower floor and start to get up. Pin pricks of pain mercilessly stab up my left arm. I fall back to the floor a gasp of pain escaping between my lips. Dammit. I'm going to need Ezekiel's help and that is the last thing I want. Hell, I hate asking for help on a good day. I don't have to ask though; he just grabs me under my arms and pulls me to a standing position.

"Can you walk?"

I don't know just been doing it since I was like two is the first response that comes to mind, but when I look up to say just that I am taken aback by how truly handsome he is. His hair is thick, wavy, and so dark it is nearly black. It adorably curls up at his ears. He has a chiseled face; one even Narcissus would envy. However, instead of appearing like the statues of Greek gods – feminine or boyish – his five o'clock shadow compliments every outline and gives him a rugged and dangerous look. Ezekiel's lips are full and decidedly kissable, but his eyes, his eyes are mesmerizing, intoxicating, like two vibrant green orbs looking into my very soul. So, when I go to speak I just can't. The sarcastic comment dies on my lips and I am left to nod.

Slowly he lets go of my arms, leaving me a little empty now that he is no longer touching me. It is weird. Horrible adjective, yes, but the only one that fits. Part of me is screaming to turn around and run away as fast as I can, that he is dangerous. The other more devious part is drawn to him and urges me to get as close as I can. I am torn. Run or stay?

My choice is taken from me when I remember that I still need to get out of my bloody, wet clothes. Usually I wouldn't think twice about tracking whatever dust, debris, and the occasional blood I'd acquired that day into the halls of what served as our home, but today is different and I don't need neat freak Mackenzie worrying about anything but caring for Annabelle. Ignoring Ezekiel I turn my attention to the button of my jeans. My fingers keep fumbling and I can't get a good enough grip to get the button through the hole. My frustration isn't helping either and I all together give up on trying to get the button through the hole and try to just pull down my jeans as they are. That doesn't work either.

"Here, let me."

I haven't a clue what he is talking about, that is until he pulls me forward by the belt loops of my jeans. He means to unbutton my pants. My pulse leaps and my heart beats a little faster. I have to remind myself that he is only helping me out of necessity and on top of that this guy bothers me. He has a dangerous air about him, one that stems from his insatiable curiosity. A lot like me, but I push that thought down. But still despite the reminder my nerve endings explode every time his hand grazes my lower stomach in his effort to undone the stubborn button. Ezekiel finishes with the button quickly and deals with my zipper too. Pushing down the heat growing in the pit of my stomach I mumble out a thanks, before he turns me around and goes to work on the clasp of my bra.

"If you can't get the button, you certainly won't be able to get this." His voice is completely normal, maybe even a little smug, like he knows how much this is affecting me, but it isn't affecting him at all. Bastard.

Just like with the button every single damn time his hand brushes across my upper back my nerve endings explode. It takes every vestige of self-control I contain to not turn around, pull my body flush against his, and kiss him for all it's worth. And again, he is seemingly unaffected. I'm not a particularly vain person, but for reasons I can't place it irritates me beyond anything that I am here doing everything I can to keep my hands off of him and he doesn't care.

He is done with the clasp in seconds, sooner than I thought he would be, and I have to slap my arm across my chest to prevent my bra from slipping off. Bra secure I turn to face him.

"Thanks, but you need to," I motion for him to turn around with my finger. He makes no argument and I am grateful despite the little tweak of irritation I get for whatever reason. I really don't want him or anyone to see my scars. He's probably already seen the horrible ones on my shoulders and that in itself makes me sick. It surprises me that he doesn't ask about them seeing as how interested he was by the others. Maybe, just maybe, I'd gotten lucky and for once my untamable curls had done something to help me, like mask the white scars on my shoulders with their black as night hue. One could hope.

As quickly as I can manage I slip out of my soaked jeans and panties. Ezekiel, either having peeked or hearing my jeans hit the floor, chooses that moment to hand me one of the big, fluffy white robes we keep folded on a shelf in the bathroom. My guess is the latter of the two, judging by how unaffected he is.

Robe on I walk out of the bathroom, fully expecting Ezekiel to follow me. Again, I am split, part of me hoping he'll follow, another part praying he'll stay put.

Disregarding all that he strikes me as the curious sort who wouldn't pass up the chance to see my room and learn more about me. He won't learn much.

To speak of the feelings that churned

inside was a death sentence. The pain

blindsided her and the rage bubbled up.

Each memory was an open wound, festering

with infection. Dwelling on them was

pouring salt. Excruciating.

Chapter 2

My room is about a thirty foot straight shot from the bathroom and a left to the doors of the library. Once through the double doors you are faced with two choices. The first is what had been the computer room for all the students that went here and Dylan's obsession for months until he "deduced" we were off the grid. The only devices he was able to get up and running were our cell-phones, but long range calls was another issue. The second room in the library used to be a study room of sorts, littered with bean bag chairs, until I cleared them out and made it my room.

I step through the beaded curtain that serves as my door and wait. Wait for the familiar *swish* of the wooden beads as they move over fabric and the *click-clack* as they fall back into place. Each sound telling me Ezekiel has followed me, just as I knew he would. I try to look at everything with the critical eye Ezekiel is bound to be using. And again, I'm taken aback, but also happy, about how little my room says about me, at least in the personal sense. One could easily deduce by the location of my room, the books sprawled across my bed, and the back wall by my head board covered with words and definitions -- currently about the Apocalypse -- that I enjoy reading and learning. To the left of the door there are hooks holding weapons of various types. Everything from maces to nunchucks. Okay I like weapons. That isn't overly surprising nor does it stand out considering where and how I live. My room isn't a pigsty nor is it OCD neat. Nothing to learn there. The few personal items I have are placed on either night stand by the head of my bed. On the right side, if you were lying down, there is a framed picture of my Papa holding a toddler version of me and my Mama looking at both of us adoringly. Hanging from the corner of the picture is Mama's locket, open and displaying a picture of Papa the day he graduated from the police academy. Sitting in front of the picture is Papa's SJPD badge. I inherited these items from Mama when she committed suicide shortly after Papa was shot and killed in the line of duty. Quickly I look away from some, if not my most prized possessions, so I won't break down. That is the last thing I need right now.

Sitting on my other night stand are two framed photos and a couple more personal possessions. In the frame surrounded by flowers is a picture of Annabelle and I at ages twelve and fourteen the day we found out John and Emily were adopting us. We'd both spent years, Annabelle longer than I, bouncing from foster home to foster home, we'd never even imagined a day would come when we'd get to stay in one place for good, but here were these two amazing people offering to adopt us. It had been so surreal. They had wanted us to be able to go and finish high school in one place. They liked us and saw potential in us, and we liked them too. John and Emily were the second people I ever called my parents. The second frame is a simple with a picture of the four of us- Annabelle, me, Mom, and Dad- caught laughing, the white, fluffy balls on our Santa hats bouncing around crazily. It had been our Christmas card that year, and one of my favorite pictures of the four of us. The personal items consist of my Dad's Bible and my Mom's cross lying over the top of it. Both of them had died over a year ago.

But Ezekiel won't be able to tell any of that from the items. Hell, he probably hadn't put two and two together and realized that though my Mama was of Mexican descent and Papa Native American and I obviously some kind of European mix that they were my parents. Biological or not they would always be my parents. All he could get from these pictures is that I loved them and since he hadn't seen them they probably weren't here.

No, he hadn't learned much other than the fact that I enjoy reading and have a some-what unhealthy obsession with weapons and that is just fine by me. The less he knows the better. I don't like the way he makes me feel, on edge, but wanting more.

Before turning to face him, I bury the emotions thinking about the loved ones I lost stirred in me and use my finely tuned skill of willing away tears before they can overwhelm me. Once the tears that dare form in the corner of eyes are dead and gone I finally turn around. Staying silent I wait from him to speak. The silence becomes awkward very, very quickly, but still I don't say a word. He had followed me and he is the one standing in *my* doorway. If he has something to say, he'll say it with no goading from me. It takes him a whole two minutes before he clears his throat and speaks. "You need stitches."

Stitches? Shit, how had I forgotten that I'd gotten hurt during my fight with the incubi. My arm throbs with the reminder. I look down and notice the wound isn't that bad. I can get away with using butterfly bandages. Mackenzie will bitch that I'm not taking care of myself, but might as well save the real stitches for the ones that need them.

"Nah, it's not that bad. I'll just use some butterflies on the really bad parts." My tone is one part polite, one part obvious dismissal. He chooses to ignore the dismissal.

"Where do you keep the bandages?"

"Thanks, but no thanks. I'll do it myself." The politeness has vanished and in its place is full-fledged irritation. I am beyond exhausted; both physically and emotionally, not yet dressed, in need of bandages, and the most important person to me is on their death bed. I am so not in the mood for a hero and that is exactly what this guy is trying to be. And besides all that I don't need a hero. Never have, never will.

He matches my irritated look with one of his own, but quickly composes himself. "Do you need anything else?" His tone is nothing but polite, further irking me.

Ezekiel doesn't strike me as a guy who gets told no, especially by girls, and I am tempted to say no simply to watch the composure slip from his handsome face, but decide it will be so much more entertaining to send him on an errand for me. A satisfied smirk settles across my face.

"Yes." This time instead of irritated he is pleasantly surprised. That will soon change, "could you get Mackenzie for me?" An innocent enough request to not seem suspicious, but Mackenzie will bombard him with questions like *"is she okay", "where is she", is she breathing", "is she bleeding"* hell she'll probably even ask if I'm alive. Doesn't sound like a death sentence I know, but believe me it is both time consuming and beyond annoying. Yes, Mackenzie out of ten is a fifteen on the worry-wart scale. That number will sky rocket to like a billion when Ezekiel tells her I am asking for her. I loved the girl, I did, but in a crisis she is no help, unless you are on bed-rest, dead, or not awake like Annabelle. And no one is stupid enough to ask for her help during a crisis. Well that is no one but sweet, helpful Ezekiel.

"Yeah, of course. I'll send her straight here." Yeah, right. He'll be lucky if he gets rid of her within the hour. Again, she's not great in a crisis. Most people know not to keep a person asking for help waiting but not Mackenzie.

"Thanks." Even if I am sending him to death by irritation, I was raised to be polite so I use my manners.

He leaves without another word, leaving me alone, a blessing and a curse. Yay! I'd finally gotten rid of the guy, so why wasn't I more happy? Maybe because now I am left with only my thoughts. Yes, Ezekiel had proven to be more curious than I'd thought when I targeted him as my distraction, a welcome distraction it was, but now with him gone there is nothing to latch on to. No irritation. No crazy suspicions or anger. I will be the first one to admit my suspicions may have been unwarranted, but they helped. For a little while longer I was able to push down the emotions that threatened to overwhelm me. Engulf me! They are coming now. I can feel them, but I can't stop them. My knees buckle under me and I plop on my bed. Huge, soul-wrenching, hiccupping sobs pour out of me. Tears run down my face as I picture Annabelle's unconscious, blood-soaked form. She is all I have left and I am tired of losing people, so fucking tired. Papa, Mama, Mom, and Dad I've lost them all. Every single one of them. I can't lose Annabelle too. I'll be alone, so utterly alone. And broken. The only reason I am able to remain positive is because of Annabelle. I stay strong for Annabelle and if she dies I'll be lost with no reason to live or go on. Dramatic? Maybe, but it is also the truth.

But through all this paralyzing grief there is a sliver of hope. No one has come to talk to me about her. That means one of two things: either they are still working on her, which means she at the moment is still breathing, or she is dead and they are waiting until I am more mentally and emotionally stable to break it to me. The latter of the two is the most likely possibility. They care about me and know that if I find out right now, in my state of partial drunkenness and all-encompassing grief, that I'll do something stupid. Not kill myself, not exactly. More like if I get in over my head with a few hellions it wouldn't be a total accident or surprise. But that sliver of hope, I hold on to it with everything I have. It is the light at the end of the tunnel, the one that keeps me from going mad and sinking into the darkness.

Sobs continue to wrack through my body. I inch further onto my bed, lay on my side in the fetal position, and wrap my arms around my waist as tightly as I can, trying desperately to make the hurt stop. Every millimeter of my body is alive with grief. It is weighing down on me, suffocating the very life out of me and I just can't stop it. Try as I might I can't stop the flow of tears that are cascading in steady streams down my face. I can't stop the hiccupy sobs from tearing out of my body, rendering me totally speechless.

Arms curl around my own, holding me tight. A hand brushes the damp hair out of my face. Mackenzie. It has to be. I hadn't even heard her come in over the noise I am making.

"It's okay. It's okay. Just breathe, Leila. Breathe." She repeats this over and over again like a mantra until it works.

Eventually my body stops shaking with sobs, the tears halt, and I am able to speak coherent words. "Kenz, I can't lose her. I can't." The despair in my voice breaks my own heart. I sound like a ghost of myself with a voice made hoarse from crying.

"You won't. Leila she's not dead." Her voice is firm, but we could both hear the doubt, it is all in the way she phrases it; she's not dead. Rather than she's alive. Yet is the word that should be tacked onto the end of that statement. Annabelle may not be dead, but she certainly isn't alive. Still that unspoken word: yet, sets my heart aflame with hope. It grows larger and brighter until it smothers just a little bit of the grief. A little bit, but enough to make my breaths come easier.

Mackenzie notices the change and quickly realizes now is the only chance she'll have to get me out of this bath robe and into some pajamas. And she does just that. Kenz walks over to my dresser and rummages through it until she finds a pair that matches. Like it matters. While throwing the set of pj's and some underwear at me she walks over to my bedside table, opens it up, and pulls out my brush.

Once dressed Mackenzie orders me to lie down and tucks me under the covers. She even goes so far as to grab the multicolored throw-blanket at the end of my bed and put that on me too. Now that that is done she is all business, telling me to lie on my side and shit, but I know what she is going to do and in that moment I am so glad Annabelle and I had decided to bring her in on the tradition as we liked to call it.

You see when I was real little, barely four, I used to get crazy anxiety. It didn't help that my Papa was a police officer.

Every single day I'd worry as each minute went by, wondering when my Papa was coming home, if he was coming home. Even with as young as I was I wasn't naïve, I knew Papa's job was dangerous. Mama used to tell me he was a superhero fighting bad guys, that didn't help. So, Papa devised a plan. Each day, depending on whether or not he had more paperwork or not he'd draw me a clock and on it the hour hand and the minute hand would be pointed to where it would be on our clock when he got home. If he was just a minute late I'd freak myself out worrying. Mama used to lay me in her lap and brush my hair. Without saying a single word she managed to calm me. It turned into our thing and it worked. Papa always ended up not more than ten minutes late. That was until the day he didn't show up at all.

When Annabelle and I had been "sisters" long enough I brought her into mine and Mama's thing. Only this time I did the brushing and Annabelle did the calming down. It went like this for the longest time. Annabelle would get worked up or angry for whatever reason and I'd lay her down and brush her hair. This changed only very recently. I had been the one to find Mom and Dad's bodies. It had been horrendous sight. There was no other word for it. They were lying on the living room floor, a look of pure fear etched into their faces forever. Mom had huge bloody scratches all down her neck, like she'd been suffocating and so desperate for air that she'd scratch open her own throat to get it. Dad didn't have any outer injuries, and when the M.E. did her examination she found no internal injuries to explain their deaths. I didn't understand any of it. I do now. A wraith had gotten to them, terrified them, and fed off their fear until they died.

Never mind the horror story that is my life, the point of all of this is that that horrible day that will forever be engraved in both my heart and mind is the first day Annabelle took care of me. At fourteen she laid a sixteen-year-old me in her lap and brushed my hair while I let out all the tears I'd bottled up during the detective's initial investigation.

We met Mackenzie and Cara Marie months later and immediately brought them into the tradition. In this new and dangerous world we lived in there was no time to waste. This brought comfort to all of us, though tough, badass Cara Marie would never admit it.

Starting at the ends of my hair Mackenzie brushes the knots out. Understanding it is more of a calming thing she takes her time. Eventually as I lose count of how many brush strokes my limbs go limp, my breathes deepen, my eyelids become heavy, and I start drifting off to the wonderful world of sleep. It is a welcome reprieve from the day I've been having. For at least a solid ten hours I'll be able to forget about everything. The crash. The blood. The certain death. Each and every one of those horrible things will be just a distant memory compared to the blanket of sleep that will soon cocoon me. In the morning they'll still be there, begging for me to break down, but tonight all there will be is blissful nothingness.

Curling deeper into my mattress I let me droopy eyelids shut. Sleep is right around the corner when Mackenzie decides to stop brushing and get up. Repressing a groan, I start to get up too and tell her to come back, that I'm not asleep yet, but his voice stops me. Ezekiel and Mackenzie are right outside my room, speaking in hushed voices. I strain my ears, trying to hear what they are talking about, all the while keeping up the appearance that I am asleep. The words are muffled but I can make out some of it.

"She asleep?" Ezekiel, obviously, because why would Mackenzie ask that.

"Yes."

"She's almost all healed. She's getting….." Can't get the rest of that sentence.

"….know. But how can that be her…….is months away…. shouldn't…. happening…. quick."

Okay I am officially lost and now my body is begging for sleep. My eyes are refusing to stay open. My ears refusing to listen. Sleep is dragging me under. Moments ago, I would've leaped, arms wide open, into sleeps arms, but now, no. Something deep in the pit of my stomach tells me I need to hear what Ezekiel is going to say. That whatever he is going to say is important to me, but I can fight sleep no longer. It washes over me like a tidal wave, taking with it, all my senses.

A twisted labyrinth lay before me –

full of dark corners and ghosts of the past

Fear lurks behind every bend

Doubt lays in wait through every door.

Hate rains from the sky

and Jealousy causes the ground to tremble.

My own little inferno – the Mind.

Once inside there's no end to be seen...

Chapter 3

I wake up to a pounding headache, courtesy of my drinking binge last night, an empty stomach, and the smell of instant coffee. My head wants to continue lying in bed but my ravenous hunger and the aroma of coffee beckoning me forward gets the best of me. Throwing off my blankets, I jump out of bed before I can change my mind. Not bothering to change, or do something with my hair I follow the smell, with one quick detour. In spite of my stomachs loud, whale-like protests there is a stop I need to make.

Each step I take brings me closer to my own personal nightmare. Too quickly I am outside the doors of what had once been the school's infirmary. Now it serves as our emergency room. You need stitches, you come here. Coma, you come here. Infection, you come here. Basically anything that is possibly life threatening is treated in this little room. There are two wooden bunk beds fitted with sheets and blankets if needed. The kids who went to this school probably used them for nap time. We use them because we are too injured to wobble to our rooms or because Mackenzie gives us no other choice.

Annabelle is in one of those beds right now no doubt. But she is either in a bed covered to her neck, I.V. in her arm, pale, sleeping, healing, and alive or she is dead, a white sheet covering her, stained red in places from blood, no movement what so ever. If the last possibility is fact then I'll lose it, even the thought of it makes the grief that has been parading around my heart constrict. Again, for the billionth time it seems in a twenty-four to thirty-six-hour period I'm having a panic attack. My heart is beating out of my chest, my lungs refuse to take in air, and I can't take this anymore. I need to know what is through that door. Forcefully I push myself forward and make myself look and face what is in that room.

Oxygen breaks the barriers my panic attack raised and I am able to breathe again. She is alive! Her tumble weed wheat-blonde hair is a mess and it is the most beautiful thing I've ever seen. Annabelle is paler than usual, something we all doubted was possible, but there is a flush in her cheeks that speaks of life. Those gorgeous corn flower blue eyes of hers are covered by her eyelids, but I know when she awakes they will light up with her tenacity to live. A tenacity that proved itself important this past day.

Resisting the urge to run toward her sleeping form and hug her with everything in me I leave and again follow the delicious aroma of instant coffee. The closer I come to the cafeteria more scents mix with that of the coffee. There are pancakes, syrup, peanut butter, and bacon. Someone has made my favorite breakfast! High on happiness I skip the rest of the way to the breakfast that awaits me. Once through the double doors I am met by the smiles of everyone I love; Rudy and his sister Cara Marie, Dylan next to her, a moody Liath red hair in his eyes sitting all alone, Mackenzie as usual in the kitchen, my heart swells with joy. My usual moody morning self is gone, and before coffee which in itself is a miracle. In her place is the loving girl I used to be, before all this death and destruction had entered my life. The loving girl would eventually disappear behind the wall I'd built to protect myself, but while she is here I'll embrace her. So, I smile right back at them, even Ezekiel who is helping himself to a cup of coffee, walk over to Rudy, and give him a big squeeze from behind.

With my head resting on his shoulder I graciously thank him. "Thanks! You even made everything just the way I like it: four pancakes with not too much peanut butter or too much syrup, three pieces of bacon on the side, and a big cup of coffee!"

"Morning breath, Medusa."

"I think the words you were looking for are 'You're welcome'."

Rudy chooses to ignore me and instead grasps my forearms, his way of hugging me back. Knowing it will only partially bother him I give him a big smooch on his cheek and sit down to devour my food. I don't open mouth to do anything but take another bite until I have licked my plate clean and tossed back two cups of coffee. And when I do speak again the first words out of my mouth are another thanks for Rudy.

"It was no big deal. I just threw the food in the microwave."

I can't help but roll my eyes at his obliviousness. "I'm not thanking you for the food. I'm thanking you for Annabelle."

This time he rolls his eyes. "You should know better than that," my confusion must show on my face because he elaborates, "no thanks needed. We love her too."

All I can do is smile. Annabelle and I have truly found a family and a home with these people. We aren't a typical family, not a one of us looked alike but for Rudy and Cara Marie who both have the most beautiful mocha colored complexion and eyes, Cara's eyes have caramel swirls running through them while Rudy has honey colored swirls; Liath is red-haired with grassy green eyes, Mackenzie has long dirty blond hair, hazel-ish green eyes, and a killer tan, Dylan has jet black hair and storm grey eyes, Annabelle has beautiful wheat-blonde wavy/ kind of curly hair with beautiful corn-flower blue eyes, and I well I have long, thick, untamable black as night curly hair and ice blue eyes. Annabelle used to say they looked like blue fire.

Each of us has a different ethnic background too. Again, Rudy and Cara Marie's is the same, they are an African American Mexican American mix. Something that shows itself in Cara's gorgeous thick dark brown hair. Liath is so obviously Irish. Mackenzie is definitely the typical white surfer chick. Dylan is Asian and white; he calls himself Whasian. Annabelle is white and Puerto Rican. And I don't know what the hell I am. We think I'm some kind of European mix. But in spite of all our differences there is one thing that bands us together: we are all survivors.

Each and every one of us went through something traumatic in our lives before all hell broke loose. Rudy and Cara Marie's dad died in battle and their mom hadn't made it through Cara's birth. They lived with their Grandmother who eventually, from old age, passed away. Rudy joined the army and Cara let the grief of her part in her mother's death swallow her whole.

Liath's mom was a notorious drug addict. The woman couldn't even stay clean to take care of her only child and instead left him to fend for himself often. Inevitably she died from an overdose of heroin, leaving Liath alone at the ripe age of thirteen. He's been living on the streets ever since then.

How Mackenzie turned out so loving we could never guess because since she was a baby she was bounced from one family member to another, each with their own excuse of why they could no longer keep her. From the start her mom hadn't wanted her, but couldn't bring herself to do the right thing and put her up for adoption where a loving family could take care of her and love her.

Now Dylan, out of all of us he probably had the easiest life when it came to money and material objects, but his family were drug lords and they wanted him to follow in their footsteps. He refused and was shunned. That's how he and Liath met. Liath's mom bought her heroin from Dylan's family. Both of them had a past they no longer wished to be a part of and they survived the mean streets of West Oakland together.

Annabelle's back story, a hard one for me to think about. Her dad was an abusive son of a bitch. He was an angry drunk that took it out on his wife and kid. His wife didn't do a damn thing about it and Annabelle suffered. One night after beating his wife to near death he called the cops on himself and Annabelle was taken in to custody by CPS and ended up in a foster home where we met.

We all voted and most traumatic back story goes to *moi*. Given up at birth, father killed in the line of duty, mom hangs herself, bounced around in foster care, finally adopted only to lose another set of parents. Yep, it's official, I win. Those are our back stories, each horrible, some worse than others, but we all survived. Some of us with someone to lean on other's all on our own. It's because of our horrible childhoods that we are all strong enough to survive Hell showing up on our doorsteps. Literally.

"You've been trying to gouge out your eyes again." Leave it to Cara Marie to ruin my moment of pride for the gang and my overall chipper mood. "You've been scratching at your wrists as well. Another nightmare?"

Her matter-of-fact tone and her pointing it out quickly sets my blood on fire. "No, it's nothing." Deflection, a useful technique, especially when the other person is right.

"Nothing?!" Cara scoffs. "Have you seen yourself?"

"No, unlike some people I don't live in front of a mirror!" Neither does she, but I am angry and can think of nothing else to say.

"You look like a tiger attacked your face."

Blood rushes to my face and I clench my teeth to hold back the vile words that are on the tip of my tongue.

"Leila, it's really not that bad," whispers Liath. Forever the peace keeper.

Cara isn't done though and the peace cannot be kept. "A week of chores says you have them on your ankles again too."

I ignore her, because I and everyone else, aside from Ezekiel, knows she is right. Since the moment this Apocalypse started I'd had horrible nightmares. In the morning, what they are about escapes my mind, but I know and everyone else knows they are nightmares, because I'd either wake up screaming or I'd wake up with scratches on my eyes, wrists, and ankles. Cara's theory is that in the nightmare I am bond at the wrist and ankles and whatever is playing out in front of me is either so gruesome or devastating that when clawing my way out of the bindings fails I resort to gouging out my own eyes instead of watching. A twisted theory for sure, but it's all we had.

"C'mon, just show me your ankles."

"No."

"Afraid to lose?"

"No, I just don't feel like showing you my ankles."

"Well then tell me what your nightmare was about." She knows I don't know, I never do, but she pushes anyways.

Between clenched teeth I spit out, "I don't know."

"How can you not know?"

"I just don't."

"C'mon, Leila, tell me. Just tell me." Each word she speaks brings my anger up yet another notch. "Just give it a guess."

I slam my fists on the table, startling everyone, stand up and yell, "I don't know! Okay?! Just fucking drop it!"

I am seething, my hands are balled into fists, and my blood is boiling. Cara is just being Cara, she pushes that's how she gets answers, but today for reasons that elude me, typical Cara Marie is setting my blood on fire.

Everybody in the room has a deer-in-headlights-look, they are afraid of me. While minutes before that would have bothered me, right now I could care less. I turn, step over the chair I had toppled in my fit of unmerited rage, and make a beeline for the door. The door I had moments earlier skipped through with joy, now I am ready to pummel someone.

The sound of the door slamming shut echoes down the hall, almost masking the sound of sneakers scuffing linoleum. Rudy has sent someone after me. Wondering who is on Leila Watch I turn to find Ezekiel by my side. "Shit! You startled me."

"Sorry."

"So, you're my babysitter for the day?"

A suggestive grin spreads across his face. "Do you need one?"

"I don't think so, but Rudy would disagree." I am too angry to even think about flirting back.

"What'd you do?"

"What?"

"To earn yourself a babysitter."

"Oh." I launch into my very biased explanation, "Well a girl gets a little overwhelmed and decides the bag ain't cutting it. So, she thinks there are perfectly good demons outside waiting to be slaughtered," here he interrupts me.

"I'm guessing you went to slaughter those waiting demons." He smiles.

I smile back. "Of course! So anyway, the gang gets worried when they can't find me. They went on a search and blah blah blah until they found me hacking away at a pack of Hellhounds, bodies of already dead hellion's littering the floor and Rudy loses it!"

Ezekiel feigns seriousness. "You can't blame him for losing it. You left the fortress."

I stifle a laugh, after all I am supposed to be mad. "Keep in mind I was winning!"

"Oh, I don't doubt it. You proved you can handle your shit last night." Instinctively or on purpose, his hand goes up to his split lip. It looks bad, blue and purple in places and the size of a small bouncy ball.

I feel a twinge of guilt. "Did I ever apologize for that?"

"I don't believe you did." He waits expectantly, a smirk on his face.

"Good, I never apologize for kicking someone's ass."

"Ouch."

Once more, I find myself trying to keep a smile off my face. "Egos aside," here Ezekiel dramatically stumbles back, hand over his heart as if I wounded him. I roll my eyes and continue, "If you're going to be tagging along you might as well make yourself useful."

Ezekiel's whole demeanor changes. He steps close to me, invading my personal space, we are toe to toe and I am forced to look up. Before when I was slightly drunk I'd been mistaken; his eyes weren't a vibrant green, they were much like mine, tiny green flames and they were flickering with....was that want?

"And how may I make myself useful?" His voice is pitched low, rough with want, this time I am sure of it.

Unsure what to do. Unsure what my pulse quickening like some internal race is going on inside my veins, my palms sweating, and butterflies attacking my stomach mean I abruptly do an about face and hurry to the bathroom. I slow down only long enough to tell a now sure to be dazed and confused Ezekiel to meet me in the weight room.

Her wall was built from

years of human failings,

cruel words and nights

spent crying.

Only behind it did she

feel safe from a world

where it's dangerous to

be different.

Chapter 4

"Idiot. Idiot. Idiot." It is the only word I can seem to get through my clenched teeth. Pacing the expanse of floor in front of the sink and mirrors I berate myself for letting a guy get to me. A year away from normal, human interactions and flirting turns me into freakin' seventh grader! Ugh! I hadn't been good with it Before, but now I am terrible. Don't misunderstand me, despite my lack of flirting skills or rather no skills present whatsoever, I'm not totally inexperienced. I've had a make-out sesh or two.

Understanding people and fitting in just never came easy to me. I was a lone wolf by choice and not because I was shy or an easy target, well not in the traditional sense; no pimples, glasses or lanky arms and legs. Whoever's gene pools I am picking from is more than generous.

I look at myself in one of the many mirrors lining the wall now, ignoring the scratches that sure enough are on my eyes I seriously look at myself. While my complexion isn't alabaster white like Belle's, my unruly ebony curls are still shocking against the slight olive tone. My face works well with high, pronounced cheekbones, a strong yet at the same time delicate nose, and perpetually pouty lips; ones I love and hate with equal measure. I am gifted with bountiful curves, accentuated on my 5'3" size 3 frame. My most startling feature, however, are my eyes. Annabelle hadn't lied when she called them blue fire. They burned, flared, and flickered with my emotions.

So, no I had no reason to be shy or hide, but I did anyway. You get enough envious verging on hateful glares from girls and decidedly disgusting lustful stares from guys and sinking into the background sounds like Heaven.

By sophomore year I was done and an over-sized hoodie became my best friend along with a pair of sunglasses to hide my eyes and hair down to hide my face. I hated attention. Belle didn't though. She was just as naturally beautiful, maybe more so, but in a softer less severe way and she reveled in it. Something that used to be my only worry.

"Fuck!" I curse myself for letting Ezekiel get me so off track. He zaps away my anger when he is around and now has it elude me when he isn't.

Most people would love that, to have someone who can quell your anger and all other emotions deemed bad, but not me. Much like Belle reveled in her beauty and the attention it brought, I revel in my anger. It fuels me. It lights my fire. Makes me push harder, train longer and rest less. Anger gets shit done.

Anger means you are alive. It means you haven't been defeated and I will not let anyone take that from me. That in mind I shuck off my pajamas, quickly brush my teeth, pull up my hair, and dress in my work out clothes. Briefly I mull over the shorts I usually wear option or the sweats that would cover my scars and decide I have been done hiding for a while now and that isn't about to change.

Minutes later I stalk into the weight room like a predator after its prey. My prey being my anger, and I will not deal with my anger Ezekiel's way, no I'll deal with it with good old-fashion violence. Ezekiel is waiting for me by the punching bag, smart kid or Rudy had told him, either way it is one less thing I have to deal with. As I square up to the bag Ezekiel steps behind it, steadying it. My fists fly without conscious thought. Over and over again. I barely stop to breathe. Left fist. Right fist. Round house kick. I go through the combo again and again, the sound of flesh hitting leather calming.

Mindlessly I circle the bag. Now and then changing up my stance for a switch kick. Other times rolling to avoid an invisible assailant. Only to pop back up again with an uppercut to the jaw. Feet shuffle, my next combo flies: double jab, right cross, left switch kick, right elbow. Skin tears as my elbow slides across the bag. The burn revives me.

How long I stand there whaling away at the bag, my anger slowly dissipating, I don't know. Must have been over an hour and I only stop because the leather rips releasing the sand inside. I step back, my chest heaving. The anger isn't all gone, not yet, but what am I to do with a broken punching bag. I debate a run, but quickly dismiss the idea; Rudy wouldn't let me leave the fortress even if I am just going to the track outside. What to do? What to do?

"Wanna spar?" Ezekiel fixing my problems. Great. But this time I won't make a fuss. I need to get rid of the rest of my anger.

"Sure." Pointedly I look at his attire; red flannel pajama bottoms and a grey tank, not exactly workout clothes. "You need to change?"

He simply shakes his head no and comes at me. Unexpected? Yes, but so is every damn demon crawling around outside. I side step him, grab his arm, and use his own momentum to throw him to the ground.

He thrusts his leg out, kicking my right one from under me. I fall on top of him. Thinking on his feet he flips us over so he is now in the dominate position – full mount -- pinning me beneath his weight. While he is distracted by his premature pride I hip escape until one leg is free and bring my knee up to his stomach. His reaction is immediate. Rolling off of me and onto the blue padded mat he holds his stomach and gasps for air. Jumping up to my feet I turn to face him. Ezekiel is slower getting up, understandably so, but once up he is an unstoppable force coming at me again and again. But I am an unmovable object coming at him with the same ferocity. After what feels like days we collapse to the sweat slicked mat, not caring how gross that is but focused entirely on catching our breathe. My anger finally seeps out, leaving me exhausted.

Once we suck in all the air our lungs will contain we lapse into a comfortable almost companionable silence. Ezekiel is the first to break the silence, and with an unexpected question. "So, how'd you do it?"

"Break the bag? Oh, that was nothing. It was old. I was angry."

Rolling to face me now. "Not that."

"Then what?"

"How did you stay alive? It's not like you grew up learning to kill demons." A pause. "Or did you?"

I laugh. So does he. I find laughing is easier to come by around him. There is just something about Ezekiel. He is the kind of person that when they walk into a room it lights up. His smile is the kind that isolates you. Suddenly you matter, you're important. When that smiles turned on you it's like finally belonging.

Rolling away from his unwavering gaze, I clear my throat and bring attention to the question at hand. "Grew up learning to kill demons, not so much, but it doesn't hurt to have people in your life who are all for the second amendment." People. What a simplified meaningless statement.

The people I am referring to are my Papa who had me outside shooting at soda cans with an airsoft gun since I was three, and his Police buddies who took over teaching me when my Papa died and continued even after I was put in foster care – at least for a bit--, and of course my Dad who took Annabelle and I hunting when it was season and to the gun range when it wasn't.

So, yeah, they were people in my life, but much more than that; they were my loved ones, my anchors, my rocks, but they were all gone. People is an easier explanation. Calling them anything else cracks my resolve. And from those fissures emotions leak. Everything I spent so long repressing would rush to the surface if I didn't blanket their importance with a single word.

"And how'd I do it? Sheer luck. Adrenaline. You name it! But it wasn't skill."

"I doubt that. You couldn't live through those horrible circumstances and not have skill. But tell me about it. What were those first few crazy days like?" There is no lilt or crack in his voice indicating he wants to know for less than moral reasons, like the girls back at school, it is just pure curiosity. Why not indulge him? And hey, it wouldn't hurt to finally talk about it. May even be therapeutic.

"I was at home with Belle when all hell broke loose." As thoughts flow from mind to mouth I am transported back the most challenging time I had yet to face.

⟊ ⟊ ⟊ ⟊ ⟊

"Would you turn that crap off?" Belle is on a complete boycott of all things bad and since the news is sadly like ninety percent bad news she never wants it on. Refused to listen or watch it. No one could blame her. Hearing your parents had passed away prematurely is enough bad news for a lifetime, made worse by the coroners ruling; suspicious causes. No answers could kill a girl.

"No. The news is informative and I, as a viewer, like to be informed."

Her huffing and puffing reaches me even though she is one room over.

Annabelle is angry now and here comes her signature rant, "You want to be informed? Informed of what?! Death! Rape! Murder! Robbery! And everything else that's bad in the world!"

I toss out the first rebuttal that comes to mind, it is weak and cliché, but so what, "Information is power."

"Information is crippling."

I suppose I should be more comforting, more understanding. Perhaps having already lost a set of parents and at such a young age, makes this easier to deal with. Though I highly doubt it. I'm as raw, if not more so, as I was when I lost Mama and Papa. I just have more experience hiding it. All I know for sure is that I am sick and tired of cynical, gloom and doom Annabelle taking the place of my fun loving, high on life sister Belle.

I mute the T.V.

"God, Annabelle! It's been nearly three weeks! Mom would not want you to go on like this. Hell, Dad always told you ignorance isn't bliss, so stop cutting yourself off from world and all its bad! By doing that you're robbing yourself of all that's good."

"You're one to talk! You hide from the world so you won't get hurt." True, but I can't hide from the contempt in her voice or the pain that statement causes me.

"Again."

"What?" she asks utterly befuddled, as if she forgets my past.

"Hurt again," I stress the word, "I don't hide so I won't get hurt, I hide so I won't get hurt again." I will away the tears threatening to spill, it is a skill I am good at, "but never mind. Do whatever the hell you want! Hate the world. I don't care."

I turn my attention back to the T.V. and go to unmute it, but her words freeze me.

"Mom and Dad are dead. We're leaving a place we've finally made home to move across the United States. There's some information for you." I hear the sneer in her voice. As much as I love Belle and no matter our connection, high school has changed her. She is far too into her beauty. In all honesty, she's turned into the mean girls that mercilessly tortured me and I always despised.

I whip to my feet so fast I'm surprised I don't fall flat on my face. "You think I don't know any of that? You think that's new information! Christ, Annabelle you forget too easily, willingly almost. I found their bodies! Why you were off making fun of girls just like me I was blindly waltzing into a house where our newly dead parents lay! I answered all the polices' questions. I called Aunty Ivy! And you can't even get mad at me for that. It was New York or foster care!" Annabelle is crying, but I can't stop, not yet, the floodgates are open and there is no stopping the flow of pent up emotion, "I love you Belle, but I swear I don't know you anymore. Even before when you were just like the girls I always hated I knew you, but now, no. You're letting their deaths swallow you whole."

Rant finished I leave her there, mouth gaped open, tears drying on her alabaster cheeks, and stalk to my room. Slamming the door shut I lean against it, catching my breathe. I hit my head as I fall to a sobbing heap on the floor, but the pain reverberating in my skull is nothing compared to the pain constricting around my heart. How did everything go so wrong? Why did the world feel the need to take everything and everyone from me? Annabelle may be alive, but the fissure between us is growing wider every day and now she is truly all I have left. My fists pound on the floor of their own accord. Again and again flesh smashes into carpet, until a tentative knock sounds at the door.

"Leila?" she is hesitant and in that moment I hate myself for that. I hadn't meant to lose control, "Are you crying?"

"No." The one unconvincing word comes out on a sob.

Gently she turns the knob and pushes on the door. I don't budge. "Let me in."

"Uh-uh." She can't see me shake my head, but I do so anyway.

"Don't make me barge through this door." In my mind's eye I can all but see Annabelle lifting her chin, squaring her shoulders, and standing upright, readying herself to barrel through the door I currently sit against.

Footsteps sound as Annabelle backs up, giving herself a somewhat running start. As the first heavy footstep sounds forward I roll to the side. Belle rams through the slightly open door and plummets to the floor. Anger marks her face for a split second, until she sees my face.

The dams I built behind my eyes broke, releasing three weeks of pent of tears, tears that are now forming two steady rivers down my face.

Belle shuffles over and throws her arms around me. "I'm so, so sorry! I've been such a bitch. God taking all my anger out on you."

My sobs ease up and I am able to speak. "Shh don't blame yourself, I only had a moment of weakness. I'm fine now." Lie and we both know it.

Her look readily goes from apologetic to exasperated. "You don't always have to be the strong one you know." Yep tired of always having the same conversation. Tired of my same old response.

"If I'm not the strong one who will be?" Flawed logic? For sure, but it is me. For fear that the strong one would fail or leave I became the strong one. I've lost too many strong people not to be afraid to lose more. If I was the strong one, failure was one me and I alone could insure Annabelle would not be left alone.

Annabelle's same old response comes quickly. "Me."

My response is quicker, "You're too young to bear that burden."

"And you're not?!" same counter every time. I swear we scripted this shit.

"Better me than you." That should've been the end of the conversation. Belle should've gave me a look that says you're impossible and left. She shouldn't have asked the next question. "Why don't you let the adults, the parents be the strong ones?"

The words burst out of me before I can clamp my mouth shut. "Parents die! They leave! They just aren't strong enough, so I have to be," the words taper off as the honest to God truth finally comes out. How many parents had I lost to Death's unforgiving grip? How many more people was I destined to lose? It was too much to contemplate.

A look of pure sorrow etches its way across Annabelle's features, sorrow for me, at how deep my scares run. Usually I try to hide how broken I am, but improvising the script threw me off. Patting my knee, she leaves the room. Giving me a chance to compose myself and dry the tears still falling from my eyes. She knows me well enough that she cares for me the way I need even though it goes against every fiber of her being. Space. It's what I crave.

For a minute longer I allow myself to wallow in the giant pit of grief Mom and Dad's deaths left. And then, like always, I pull myself together and leave my room to go check on Belle. Again, like always.

I'm not bitter, just tired. Being the strong one will do that to you. These past couple of weeks I've felt like Atlas with the weight of the world tempting to crush me. The weight of losing my parents had crushed Annabelle and had almost crushed me. One of us has to keep standing though and I am always that one.

"Leila!" The mix of horror and confusion in Annabelle's voice breaks through my destructive train of thought. From my room I bolt to the living room where I find Annabelle frozen in front of the T.V. screen. Slow, as not to spook her, I come to her side.

If this was a cartoon my jaw would've literally fallen to the floor, but it's not. Instead I stand still, mouth gaped open in confusion and horror. Running across the T.V. screen is live footage of the happenings in downtown. In the middle of an intersection stands a fifteen by fifteen foot gaping hole. What is odd though is if something collapsed, causing the hole, all the cars in the immediate vicinity would be piled up in the hole, instead they are scattered all about, overturned and smoking. Worse than that is pieces of what appears to be street, impaling nearby buildings. And that is only the visible destruction. How many bodies lay under the wreckage is too many to debate. What cries can be heard? If any sound at all. Too much remains unknown and it terrifies me.

A heavy layer of grayish smoke and filaments of debris cloud the rest of the image. Standing in the middle of the nightmare, dangerously close to the abysses edge is the news anchor.

She is calmly reporting on the chaos when something reaches out from the hole, grabs her ankle, and drags her down and out of sight. Annabelle and I gasp in unison. Following the reporters disappearance into

who-knows-what to who-knows-where
things start slithering, crawling, scuttling,
and in some cases flying out of the hole.

"Belle, go lock all the doors and
windows." My words shatter the silence and
breaks through the haze of our absolute
shock and befuddlement. Annabelle
hesitates for a split second before she obeys
my command.

Screw fate. And destiny.
Fuck should be's and
could be's. There is only
today and what you do with
it.

Chapter 5

For a brief moment I pull myself out of the memory, compelled to try and explain to Ezekiel the craziness of the situation.

"To this day I don't know how I knew, but it's because I knew that we're still alive. Something just felt wrong, off and deep in my gut I knew those dark slithering shapes were coming for us, for everyone. So, we prepared."

I fall back into my memory and continue with my story.

⚇ ⚇ ⚇ ⚇ ⚇

"When you're done with that strip the beds." I am all business now. Annabelle, on the other hand, is losing her mind, and at the moment babbling.

"What the hell was that! God, oh God. Why do I have to strip the beds?! What's going on? Oh for shit sakes what are those th—" I slap her, hard. She shuts up, inclines her head towards me in thanks, and lets me speak.

I give her as much as an explanation as I can. It isn't great, but it is all we have.

"I don't know what those things are, but it's not God's work that's for damn sure. As far as what's going on, nothing good. You're stripping the beds so we can use the sheets to cover the windows." Annabelle's mouth yawns open, probably to ask why. "Before you ask why I don't know, but deep in my gut I know… I feel that shits going to hit the fan. We need to barricade the house."

She doesn't move a muscle. Belle stays death still. "I can't do this alone Annabelle and it needs to be done. Barricade or die, those are our choices."

Eventually she breaks through the mental block that keeps her from believing what she plainly saw with her own eyes. Slowly and very unsure she nods. "What should I do with all the stuff?"

I breathe out a sigh of relief. "Leave the fitted and flat sheet in the rooms. Bring all the comforters and pillows out here."

She bobs her head and leaves to do as I instructed. Turning around I head for the garage.

Piles upon piles of wood; 2x4's, 3x8's, plywood in all different sizes, old fencing my Dad had been refurbishing, new doors for a project he'd been working on, and many more are neatly stacked on six five shelf industrial wood and metal shelving. To my right is an equally industrial looking work bench with surprise, surprise more wood and tools galore. Never in my life have I been so overjoyed that my dad was a carpenter.

Gathering up all the tools I put them back in Dad's tool box and make my first trip inside. Fifteen plus trips later everything but for five 2x4's, a handful of nails, and a hammer are inside.

Quick as humanly possible, I nail shut and board up the door in the garage that leads outside. After that I head back inside, close the door, and lock and board that door as well. Since this will be our escape route I only use three 2x4's and don't hammer the nails in all the way. Unless something manages to barrel through both doors, we are safe from this end. Now the front door.

Five boards nailed over it and we are good. Back door receives another five boards and I am eternally grateful we don't have sliding glass doors but a regular door with a small window. By the time I finish with the backdoor, Annabelle is ready for more instructions.

"Take the new doors and nail them long ways across the windows in all the bedrooms. When you're done with that take the fitted sheet and hang it up over the window so that it's completely covered."

This time she doesn't stop to ask frantic questions, she just obeys my orders.

Last touches on the back door; a blanket from the couch nailed over the window, now it is living room windows time. Annabelle has taken the last of the doors so it is two boards over each window. There's not enough space between the boards for a person to fit through, I can hope it will keep out whatever those things on the news are too.

Kitchen windows now. Grabbing another throw blanket from the living room, and a few more boards of wood, and I go to work in the kitchen, the last area that needs to be done.

Annabelle comes to me again. "What next?"

"C'mon, follow me." Bypassing both our rooms I cross the threshold to what had been our parent's room. Though most of their stuff is packed and in storage it still physically hurts just to be in here. Swallowing down the grief I pay attention to the now and what still needs to be done.

"Take their flat sheet and nail it over the bathroom window. Grab everything we may need and then close and lock the door." I hate the crack in my voice, the way it betrays my never-ending grief.

While she does that, I will use my impressive muscles to move their queen-sized mattress out of their room, through the decidedly narrow hallway, and lean it against the nailed shut front door.

Five minutes and some huffing and puffing later I have managed to drag the mattress to the front. Box spring time! Yay! Not.

Eleven minutes later and that too is leaning against the front door. It isn't nearly fast enough though. Sunset is coming and soon.

"Belle! Help me move yours and my mattress into the living room. We'll sleep on those."

Two mattresses in the living room later and it is box spring time…again, but it is also sunset. We need to hurry.

"Grab your box spring and I'll grab mine. We need to prop them against the back door. Now!"

Using our last bit of strength, we manage to get the box springs to the back door. Exhausted we conk out, ignoring the unfamiliar noises that fill the night.

⽊   ⽊   ⽊   ⽊   ⽊

"The next day was just as brutal. Physically. Emotionally." Remembering hurts, but now that the words fall from my mouth more wish to join.

"How so?" Ezekiel asks.

"Like deciding what we needed, what we didn't. Dividing the food, saving some for travel. Stuff like that."

Ezekiel takes in the information, looking thoughtful for a moment, and proceeds with his next line of questioning. "What next?"

"We left. Filled up my Dad's truck and went in search of more ammunition."

"Why not food?"

I had a feeling he'd ask that. "The minute we were out of the house, demons everywhere. I must've killed three just trying to get into the truck safely. At that point we needed ammo more desperately than food."

He is completely captivated, eyes solely focused on me, mouth slightly gaped open in awe. This time he has no questions. I continue.

"So, we headed to the nearest sporting goods store, hoping it wasn't completely ransacked. We never got a chance to find out. As we got out of the truck a pack of crazed looking dogs approached us." Hellhounds. I, of course, didn't know that then, but now I'd never mistake their red and yellow eyes for a normal canine. In retrospect, the black saliva dripping from their double rows of razor sharp teeth should've sent off some alarms, but my emotions had been all over the place. There was no time to truly examine the horror I faced.

"So, what did you do?" Ezekiel is like a kid at bedtime, engrossed in a story. It's cute.

"I sprinted, yelled at Annabelle to get in the truck and stay put. I didn't know about the dead end. Got surrounded. You know the rest." I don't like revisiting that day, even now a phantom pain courses through the scars I am left with. The memory of the shear amount of blood pouring from the shredded wounds makes my breakfast turn in my stomach. Time for a new subject.

"That's that."

He's still watching me, the same look of awe spread across his face.

"What?"

Snapping out of his dream like state he answers me, "You're just amazing."

Heat flows through my cheeks, coloring them bright red. How embarrassing. Ezekiel knows how to throw me off my non-existent game.

"Um…thanks."

"You're welcome."

We are still facing each other, him studying my face, me avoiding eye contact.

It begins to get real awkward when Liath saves the day.

The doors to the weight room/gym burst open, hitting the walls with a loud bang that reverberates throughout the room. Liath always underestimates his strength.

"Leila, Annabelle's awake and asking for you."

Loving you was

standing before an altar

blood pooling down the sides,

soaking the ground below, a blade

poised for the death blow,

glinting crimson in the

candle light. Being with you

was a sacrifice of who I was,

who I could be – of

my very soul.

Chapter 6

The rest of the weight that had been perched on my chest, waiting to suffocate me, subsides. A huge, toothy, genuine smile spreads across my face as I jump up, ignoring the pain all over, and run out the door Liath holds open for me, an equally big grin painted on his usually grim face.

Ignoring the stitch in my side I sprint past the faded sky blue lockers, past the wooden library doors, past the barred windows, all the way to the infirmary door. Here I allow myself to quickly catch my breath, the much needed oxygen burning its way down my throat before filling my lungs, then I burst into the room.

Belle jumps, startled, but quickly composes herself; if you can count a yip of delighted surprise and grin bigger than mine as composure, when she sees it is me.

"Leila!"

Quickly walking to her bedside I say, "Belle you're looking good!" And she is. A blush of color like the pink that paints the morning sky at dawn has flushed back into her cheeks. Her hair is still a massive tumble weed, but it still as per usual looks great. The best part, however, is the twinkle of rebellion in her eyes. Who would have ever thought I'd be happy to see that, but I am, and not just happy but ecstatic.

"I know! And you look tired."

"Trying to say I look like shit?" I ask.

"Not trying," she replies.

I snatch the pillow at the end of her bed and hurl it at her. "Well you're certainly back to your old self."

"Did you ever doubt I would be?" Sticking out her tongue, like the immature fifteen-year-old she is, Belle grabs the pillow I threw at her and she had effortlessly caught and puts it behind her head, adding it to another exceedingly fluffy pillow.

"Of course not."

"That's not what I heard," she says.

"Listening to useless gossip again?" I ask.

"I heard," she plunges ahead, completely ignoring me, "that you downed a whole bottle of vodka and showered in your clothes."

Her eyes are stretched wide like white and cornflower blue disks in mock innocence, but she can't conceal the slight upward pull of her mouth.

Hand over my heart, I stagger back, taking a page from Ezekiel's book of Dramatics. "Why I would never!" I exclaim in my best imitation of a southern accent.

She snorts. I had a feeling she didn't quite believe me. Hell, I didn't believe me. "Well maybe I was a little bit worried," I grudgingly cough up.

"A whole bottle of vodka?" she asks, eyebrows disappearing into her hairline.

"Fine a lot! I was worried a lot, but you're fine."

"I'm fine," she repeats.

I inhale a deep breath, letting the oxygen fill every inch of my lungs and then exhale; willing the rest of the lingering worry for Belle to leave my body with the breath. The moment grows uncomfortable, as it always does when we get too touchy feely. It is one thing for us to joke, like I had with Rudy this morning, but actual serious emotional talk leaves us both mute and ready for a new conversation, which Annabelle provides this time, but without knowing, she changes the subject to something more awkward.

"So, where were you?"

"What?" I ask.

"Why weren't you here waiting for me to wake up?"

"Are you so self-involved that you expected me to be waiting here?" Deflection: my favorite technique.

Annabelle sees right through me. "Everyone else came by right after breakfast. The only people who were missing were you and somebody named Ezekiel." For the umpteenth time since we began talking mock innocence paints her face, but I can identify the mischievous set of her smile; all those teeth could give the Cheshire cat a run for his money. She is making up for lost time or she is hiding something, she tends to mess with me when she's done something she shouldn't, either way I'll play along. For now.

"God, is nothing sacred!" I throw up my hands and my head back, and start pacing and mumbling: the whole shebang.

"Ooooh! Is there finally romance in the air for you?" She is in full gossip girl mode, interest at its peak. Armageddon can take the girl out of high school but it can't take the high school out of the girl.

"No, no, no. He was just my security detail and sparring partner. Oh, I also punched him in the face."

"What!?" Belle bolts up ramrod straight in bed. It is totally overkill, and exposes her true intentions as I knew it would, she is hiding something.

"Yeah, thought he was attacking me. I was wrong. So what are you hiding?" Quick fire unexpected draw questions usually trip her up, but not this time.

"Not hiding anything. Why did you think he was attacking you?"

"Subject change much?" I ask.

"No, just curious," she answers. Belle is starting to sweat though. She is avoiding eye contact and beadily looking around the room, probably searching for an escape. There isn't one. She never could lie to me for long. Now will be no different.

"I'm going to ask you one more time, okay?" she at first glance appears unfazed, but I catch her fearful swallow and downcast eyes, "What are you hiding Annabelle Delilah Wright?"

All it takes is a stern, unwavering gaze and the use of her full name and she is chirping like a bird. "I don't know. Nothing. It's just something the incubi said."

She isn't finished, but she needs some prodding. I comply. "What did the demon say?"

She hesitates a moment further, choking on words she seems to fear, before she pours it all out. "It looked at me and said Leila, but like a question. And then it got closer, so close I could make out every one of its slimy midnight blue scales and its disturbing yellow cat-like eyes and it studied me. Then it said 'Not Leila', or more like hissed it and fucking—"

"Watch your mouth."

"Sorry. And then it stabbed me with its freaky barbed tail!"

"You're one-hundred percent sure it said my name?"

"Yes."

My stomach drops like a brick. My throat plasters up. I don't know how I know this is monumentally bad but just like with the first day after the Before I just know; my safety net, the one I've been clinging to like a baby clings to its mother, has been cut and I am left dangling.

Annabelle knows it too. "We have to go! Far away. It's not safe here anymore."

To anyone else, hell especially to us, this conversation is completely irrational, verging on insane, but at the same time nothing ever made more sense.

"But go where? As far as we know everywhere else has gone to shit too."

"We don't know that though. We haven't gone much further than down town." It is a valid point, but still it's too risky.

"But again, where would we go?"

She thinks for a moment. I can tell she doesn't like the thought by the way she chews on her lip and unconsciously picks at her already ruined nails. "Umm maybe your parents?" She squeaks out the last word. That should be my first clue.

"We lived in the heart of Downtown San Jose. You know just the epicenter of the chaos explosion, but I'm sure the house is just perfect."

"Curb the sarcasm. I'm not stupid."

"You're not?" I ask a smirk drawn across my face.

Belle glares, but doesn't comment. "I didn't mean those parents. I meant your real parents."

"They are my real parents," I snarl.

"Unclench the jaw, killer, that's bad for your teeth," she replies.

"Come up with a better idea and I will."

Her demeanor changes instantly. Beads of perspiration form on her forehead. Her cheeks lose all flush of life and she is as ghostly pale as she was the night before. With hands shaking uncontrollably she stutters out, "I-I d-do-don't ha-ha-have any oth-th-er ideas."

Annabelle is afraid, deathly afraid. So I switch tactics and ease up. "I don't even know where they live."

"I do," she quickly replies, solving problems I'd rather not solved.

It takes some effort to keep the annoyance out of my voice, but I manage. Barely. "And where would that be?"

Annabelle obviously doesn't notice my struggle, because she answers, believing I am all for the idea, most chipper, "Caelo, Oregon. It's a small coastal town."

My irritation flares quickly replacing annoyance. "And may I ask how you know this?"

If it is at all possible Belle pales further becoming nearly transparent.

"When you were going through that box of your old things at Mom and Dads you threw away everything from your parents --"

"Yeah, I remember."

"I saved everything."

"That doesn't explain how you know where they live," I state, patience fading rapidly.

"I kinda looked up their address, so if you ever wanted to meet them you could."

Belle plasters on the best encouraging smile she can muster, but when it comes to my birth parents I want nothing to do with them like they obviously want nothing to do with me. "I appreciate the thought, but I have absolutely no interest in ever meeting them." Unconsciously I fold my arms over my chest, hugging myself; a defensive gesture if there ever was one.

"But they're your parents," she argues.

"Birth parents," I rebut.

Irritated and desperate, not a great combo, Belle loses it. "Well birth parents or not they're our only option! And we have to leave! You're not safe!"

"And what makes you think I'd be safe there?" I calmly ask.

"We'd only have to defend from three fronts."

"Why?"

"We'll have the ocean to our backs," she answers.

Unable to help it I scoff. "Yes, because we know from personal experience the ocean is sooo safe." Pointedly I turn 180 degrees so Annabelle will get an eye full of the twin set of scars that run the length of my legs.

"We also know from personal experience that sirens can't leave the water," Belle argues, "We'll just stay out of the water."

"Sheer genius!"

"Seriously, you can cut the sarcasm."

"What did you expect," I ask, "You're only idea involves my bio parents."

"It's the only idea we have!" she hollers and throws her hands up in the air, obviously done with me. Belle cools her temper and continues with our odd logic, "When you had a feeling that shit was going to hit the fan, I helped you board up our house. When you felt like we should leave the safety of said house, I didn't argue. We've done insane things based on your bad feelings, so now it's my turn. I have a bad feeling so we're leaving." Annabelle squares her shoulders, thrust her chin up and out, and looks me dead in the eye. She is expecting a fight. She wouldn't be getting one though, because as much as I hate it she is right.

"Okay."

"Okay?" she asks, her determined posture changing to one of befuddlement.

"Yes," I say, defeated.

"Yes," Belle repeats still slightly confused, "Okay. When do we leave?"

For the one calling the shots she sure has a lot of questions. "In a few days."

"A few days!? We don't have a few days! The freakin' demon was looking for you!"

"Belle take a chill pill. I'm aware of the situation, but you're in no shape to move. Also, we have to pack, get your bike fixed, and inform the gang of our departure."

"Oh, I forgot about that."

"What," I ask.

"The gang," she answers, "that we'd be leaving them behind."

"We can't expect them to come with us."

"But we can give them the option, right?" she hysterically asks.

"Yes, but—"

"I know," she says, broken.

With everybody she lost

    a part of her went with them

until she was nothing more

    than left over pieces stolen

from everyone she once knew...

Chapter 7

"You saw Annabelle?" Mackenzie asks from the couch placed on the other half of the cafeteria. It's our version of a living room. Schools don't typically come with one of those. We made do.

"Yeah," I answer lost in thought.

"Then why do you look troubled?"

"Do I?"

"Yes."

"Oh, no reason."

"Lie," Cara Marie interjects.

"If she says there's no reason then there's no reason." Liath coming to my defense.

Cara doesn't care for that. "Shut up, suck-up."

It doesn't help when Liath sticks out his tongue.

"You're so immature," Cara sneers.

"Ignore them," Mackenzie says while grabbing my hand. "What's wrong?"

I plop down next to her on the dangerously comfortable deep brown couch. "I'm fine." Kenzie doesn't look like she believes me. "I promise."

She holds my gaze for a minute longer, tuning out the sounds of Cara and Liath bickering, "I don't believe you, but you never did spill the beans until you were ready."

"Thank you."

"So," she begins while tugging on my sweats, "lazy day today?"

"Yep. Junk food and movies."

"No hunting?" she inquires, the ghost of a knowing smile stretching from her thin, pink lips to her beautiful green flecked hazel eyes.

"Belle made me promise," I pout. Just then Rudy comes up, flicks my bottom lip, and proceeds to lay across mine and Mackenzie's laps.

"What's up with dumb and dumber?"

"Liath's trying to keep the peace. Your sister's trying to disrupt it," Kenzie answers.

"The usual," I chime in.

"So, Annabelle's good." It isn't a question, more of a statement, but I answer anyway.

"Yeah, she's resting."

"And you?" he asks.

"Better now that Belle's off her death bed."

He grins satisfied I'll reframe from getting into trouble and asks, "Lazy day?" at the same time, just as Kenz did, he pulls on my sweats.

"Why does everyone assume it's a lazy day if I have sweats on?"

They both look at me like the answer is obvious and I am crazy if I don't see it.

"What?!"

"If it was a regular day you'd be sporting jeans, a t-shirt, and your signature combat boots," Rudy says.

"Not to mention an arsenal of weapons the military would be jealous of," Kenzie adds.

"Okay, okay I can understand the assumption and since the assumption is right, would you pretty please make popcorn?" I ask Rudy, my eyes wide, mouth pouting but this time in the form of a puppy dog face.

Rudy rolls his eyes, but gets up anyway.

"Did you get him to leave so we could talk?"

"What happened to not pushing?" I ask.

"Fine, fine you're right. I'm sorry. So what did you want to watch?"

I think for a second and I know what I want to watch but the name is eluding me. "How about that old Disney movie with the lizard, the girl with the insanely long hair, and the guy with the horse."

"*Tangled*?" Kenzie supplies the answer.

"Yes! That one. I used to watch it all the time as a kid."

"Okay, *Tangled* it is. I'll go get it."

"Thanks," I call after her.

I grab the blanket draped over the back of the couch and snuggle into it. Briefly, I wonder where Ezekiel has wandered off to, but then Rudy comes back with the popcorn and snuggles in next to me. With half-chewed popcorn in his mouth he asks, "So what movie we watching?"

"God, close your mouth," I say and give him a slight push, "*Tangled*."

"Seriously?! A princess movie?"

"There's action too," I point out.

"True but—"

"No buts, we're watching it."

"Okay."

"Way to back down, big bro," Cara teases from a red bean bag on the floor.

Liath, not knowing when to shut his mouth, interjects on Rudy's behalf, "It's called being polite. You should try it some time."

Cara jumps up from the bean bag chair so quickly it's like a movie in fast forward. I can tell by the red-ish tinge in her normally mocha brown eyes that she is aching for a fight and hoping Liath will give her one. Despite his unknowing antagonistic behavior that tends to flair around Cara he truly is the peacekeeper of the family, and he won't engage in an actual all-out fight with Cara.

"You shut your mouth or I'll shut it for you!" Cara snarls into Liath's face.

Liath is unfazed. "Real original."

For fear that Cara will rip him a new one, because she can, I jump in between them. Liath and anyone else who underestimates Cara Marie are plain stupid. Yeah, she has a willowy build, all legs and no apparent muscle, but she'd sooner rip you to shreds than back down.

"Okay, guys, we know you don't totally get along." More like not at all. Cara is an acquired taste, and Liath hasn't acquired the taste just yet. "But today's a good day, so can we please simmer down?"

"But Leila—"

"Like I told Rudy, no buts, just sit down and enjoy the show."

Because it isn't really Liath's fault, he seriously is just trying to help, I wink at him, letting him know I'm not blaming him. His shoulders hunch a little less after that. I return to my seat next to Rudy. "Thanks for all the help big bro," I mimic Cara.

He just puts his hands up in an I-surrender-gesture. "I have no control over her."

"Eh, okay, you get a pass."

"Why, thank you." Sarcasm must run in our non-blood related family.

Kenzie either having not heard dumb and dumber's argument or deciding to ignore the stupidity skips into the room, movie in hand.

"Ready everyone!!"

Mumbled yeses echo in the room, a few what are we watching joins the chorus as Dylan and Ezekiel join us.

"*Tangled*." I readily answer, expecting groans of disapproval, but get none. Instead I get Ezekiel in a blue bean bag chair by my feet. Blood rushes to my cheeks, my heart races, and when he turns his 100 watt smile on me my stomach does a stupid little flip. Freakin' biology.

100 watt smile still on me he asks, "So you like Disney movies?"

"Yeah," I answer trying to hide how uncomfortable, in a good way, I feel with him next to me.

"Disney movies," he slowly says while tapping his temple with his index finger, "I'll add that to the small list of things I know about you."

I know he is baiting me, but in that instant I want to be baited. "And what's on this list of yours?"

"You've been adopted, twice. Annabelle's not actually your sister. You're dangerously smart and intriguing. You're good with weapons and they fascinate you. You have a mean punch. You love Annabelle more than anything. You have anger management issues. You like Disney movies. And you like me."

He smiles, but I can't. He had gleaned far more information than I thought possible through one trip to my room. Observant bastard. When faced with the decision of showing him all my cards, letting him know how right he is, or putting on my best poker face, poker face wins out. Every time. "Oh I like you? You assume that why?"

"Well I'm all up in your personal space and you haven't moved over an inch. If anything you've moved closer," he answers a smirk on his face.

Had I moved closer? I look down at where I now sit and sure enough my legs are now pressed against his broad, muscular shoulder and lean side. But who moved? Me or him? It has to be him. I don't recall moving an inch.

"And how do you know I'm not just being polite?"

"Because I've met you," he replies.

I am both taken aback and impressed by his blunt honesty. Ezekiel is certainly a mystery to be solved for many reasons. First and foremost, the array of unfamiliar emotions he wakes in me every time he is near. Like now, the happiness I feel, if that is the right word, is rushing through my veins, warming me from the inside out, turning my cheeks pink. It irritates me beyond anything because I can't understand it, but I can't bring myself to move.

Arguing his reason would be futile, so I give in. "Yeah, you're right about that."

"So, you do like me then?" he pushes.

"I'm intrigued by you."

"Good enough for me."

I go to ask him what, like why and what is good enough for him, but his attention is completely captivated by the screen flashing with color in front of us. Perhaps it'd been awhile since he watched television. We are lucky to have the genius that is Dylan, not to mention solar panels, lunar panels, and a back-up generator.

Cara grabs the remote from Kenz and races through the previews, impatient. The film, the one Cara hadn't wanted to watch and I did, is scrolling across the screen in no time, but I can't bring myself to pay attention let alone watch.

All I can think about is that I am leaving all this. Leaving it all on a whim. We don't have a normal life; not by far. I've seen more decaying human bodies than I dare count, the scent of putrid, rotting flesh a stain in my memory that no amount of suppression could clean, but here I am safe. I've been hacking away at demons, arguing and loving these people with equal measure, exploring the destruction for over a year I'd be lost without the chaos. And worst of all: sitting on the couch, Kenzie on my left; Rudy on my right a big bowl of popcorn in his lap; Dylan squatting in a bean bag chair looking utterly infallible as always; Cara her perpetual bitch face etched into her features like the Ten Commandments in stone, Liath on the recliner, stubborn flaming red hair falling in his eyes; hell, even Ezekiel sitting at my feet like a loyal dog, I know they are all clueless. They are clueless, because I have yet to inform them of the greatest treachery of all; desertion. I am willingly going to desert my misfit band of soldiers to save myself. Annabelle isn't in danger, I am. We are leaving Rudy, Cara, Mackenzie, Dylan, Liath, and Ezekiel -- if he plans on staying-- to their fate. Two missing gears in an otherwise functional machine can be fatal.

The hidden truth is crawling under my skin causing an invisible rash only I can see. The itch is unbearable, swarming up my arms and down my legs like bees. I hold back from itching, partly because I don't want to open the fresh sores on my wrists and ankles and also because then I'll draw attention my traitorous way. It is a futile battle, lost before it begins. The only way to stave off the itch is to tell the truth.

I clear my throat of the frog that now resides there and say into the room silent of all things but a girl demanding to be taken to the floating lights. "Can you please pause the movie?"

At first groans and accusations that I am the only one who actually wanted to watch the movie meet me, but one look at the resignation on my face, the slight downward pull of my mouth, my heavy eyelids, and a gleam of unshed tears in my eyes and they shut up. Cara turns to pause the movie and for the first and maybe only time her face is wiped completely of the bitchyness that usually lives there. I must look bad.

Cara easily grows impatient though. "What is it Leila?" Her words hold neither anger or annoyance. They aren't meant to cut me to the bone, but I feel the slice anyway.

There is no point in beating around the bush. Not only would they see right through the tactic, it would only delay the inevitable. So, I buck up and spit out, "Annabelle and I are leaving."

I firmly shut my eyes, curl in on myself, hold my breath, and brace for impact. It never comes. No accusations or outraged remarks about my traitorous behavior. Nothing but Liath's whispered, "Why?" His voice is full of pain and it cracks on the one word. A pang goes through my heart. If I hadn't promised Annabelle we'd leave, then right now with the hurt in Liath's voice echoing in my head I'd decide to stay.

How can I possibly explain this to them in a way they'll understand? I barely understand. "It's just no longer safe for us." With a whole lot of effort I am able to keep the same pain as Liath's out of my voice. The defeated posture I wear as a second skin though, I can't help that.

Now I am bombarded with question. What and why the loudest and most frequent among the bunch. Rudy, as our unofficial designated leader, steps in to quiet the chorus. "Guys give her a second. I'm sure she has a logical explanation." His mouth says that, but his face says he is just as confused as everyone else.

I choke on the "logical" explanation, it sticks in my throat like gum sticks to hair. Mackenzie seeing the struggle that plays out on my face rushes to my side from where she has gotten up to pace and tries to soothe me.

"It's okay. Just tell us. We won't be mad."

She says that now, but it is a lie. She, all of them, don't understand that we are leaving them to whatever fate has in store for them, for me. I squirm beneath the motherly love in her. I just can't take it anymore.

"The demon said my name. The one that attacked Annabelle. I killed it, but there was blood everywhere. I thought Annabelle was gonna die, but she didn't. Then she told me it wasn't safe here. So we're leaving." The explanation bursts out of me in one indecipherable blurb.

Dylan, the guy who doesn't only decipher code from computer but also ramblings of an idiot, steps into help. He snaps his fingers in front of my face, I assume to gain my attention, and says, "Look at me."

I comply.

"Now tell me what the demon said."

"It said my name: Leila."

"How did it say it?" Dylan doesn't ask questions like Kenzie. No, he is far more clinical All work. It's not like he doesn't care. This is just how he shows it.

"Like a question," I answer.

"Then what did the demon do?"

"Annabelle says it got closer, really close and kind of inspected her."

"And?" he prompts.

"We assume it noticed she wasn't me." Dylan asking the questions the way he does helps. The love shining in Mackenzie's eyes and either the worry or confusion in everyone else's eyes would've sent me right back to babbling.

"Is that when it attacked her?"

"Yes," I answer.

"And now Annabelle believes it's not safe for you here?"

"Yes," I repeat.

"Okay."

"Okay?" I sound like Annabelle now, when I had agreed to leaving.

"Yeah, okay."

"That's it?"

"I'm done, I don't know about everyone else."

Like before, I expect to be bombarded with questions, but none come from the sea of worried and confused faces. In a way that is worse. They aren't mad, they are hurt, and their hurt is suffocating me. I jump up from where I sit almost sending the popcorn flying everywhere in the process, mumble out an excuse and leave.

Already my good mood has vaporized. I don't know what is up with me. These past couple days I've been acting completely out of character – crying, beating up a stranger, fleeing (twice) – it is ridiculous and beyond annoying. I resist the urge to punch the lockers lining the walls and growl instead.

I pace the ugly cream tiled hallway, debating another go at the bag, but then remember I broke the only one we had left and besides all that I am exhausted. The bag now no longer an option I head toward my room to do homework. The end of the world is no excuse for stupidity.

Dylan calling out my name stops me in my tracks. Briskly, I jog back to where I had just been and where he now stands. I try to read him, but his face gives away nothing.

"What's up, D?"

As usual he wastes no time with transitions or anything that would make whatever comes next easier to swallow. He is all business with one objective in mind; deliver the news.

"I'm coming with you."

I do that gesture people do, the one where you kind of wiggle your finger in your ear, because you're not quite sure you heard them right. It's more of a show than helpful, but I just can't resist. There's no way Dylan doesn't see me do it, we are like two feet away from each other, but he waits patiently anyway, practically ignoring me. Okay, verbal response it is.

"I'm sorry, I don't think I heard you right."

"I'm coming with you," he repeats, "so is Liath."

"Dylan, you guys can't come with us," I calmly state. It's that or delve into the panic that takes hold at his words.

"Who's going to stop us," he asks just as calmly.

Forcing the anger that starts to rise back down I reply, "Your conscience."

"That's precisely why we're going with you," he shoots back.

"No, that's why you should stay. These people need you and your brains, not to mention your uncanny ability to fix nearly everything. They'll be lost and in danger without you." The fact is that they'd be lost and endangered without Annabelle and me too. Each of us plays an important role in making whatever it is we have here (safety?) work. Rudy is the charismatic leader. Mackenzie the (s)mothering type. Dylan is the brains. Liath the peacekeeper. Even Cara has her role, the bitch who is one hell of a shot and loyal like a dog…she fights like one too. Annabelle, well Annabelle, is the quiet kid you don't know has it in her to wreak vengeance on any demon who dares show their face. And me, I am the loose cannon, in many cases the strongest, but also the most dangerous.

Proof of my tendency towards dangerous behavior is the fact that Annabelle still lies in a bed, still pale, and still on the mend. So maybe the gang could get along without me and my reckless ideas. Perhaps they could do without Belle, who in her own vengeance seeking way is dangerous too. But there is absolutely no way they'll make it without Dylan. His brains keeps us in contact when we are out in the field. His brain gives us warm water and food. His brain keeps our battered vehicles running. And if he takes Liath with him, everyone is doomed. Without Liath we'd do the demons a favor and kill each other.

Knowing I am right Dylan switches tactics. "There's no way Liath will just let Annabelle leave, at least not without him."

He has a valid point. Belle and Liath aren't official or anything, but who are they kidding? She is head over heels and he is whipped. In planning our departure, I neglected to take their undying teenage love into account and so too did Annabelle. Or did she? A question to ponder later. Right now, I have to deal with an incessant Dylan. Blah.

"Well he'll just have to deal." Bad cop is my only option. Honestly, I can't stop them from coming with, and as much as I'd love them to come, I just can't bring myself to agree.

Dylan steam rolls over my hard ass comment and goes for the kill shot. "We both owe you."

"You owe me nothing." In my mind they don't, but in theirs I am an angel who saved their behinds.

"Liath and I would be dead or worse if you hadn't gone all Katniss on those hellions." Point proven, but still.

"Katniss doesn't use a cross bow."

Dylan loses the reins on his temper long enough for his words to come out on a growl, "Not my point."

I know that so I move back to his original comment, "Sooo? Everything you do, everyday makes up for that."

"It won't ever be enough," he says solemnly.

I can't argue with this Dylan. His feelings are his feelings and I can't change those. So what if like eleven months ago on one of my many scavenger hunts/killing expeditions I ran into two half-starved kids. So what if when I found them they had a pack of nasty yet-to-be named hellions on their asses. And so what if I killed those hellions and brought those half-starved kids into our safety net. They would've done the same for me. Cause becoming lost, rapidly, I decide I am not beneath begging. "D, it's dangerous and chaotic out there. Annabelle can barely walk, none of us have been outside the city limits in forever, let alone Cali, and we could die. Please, please don't put yours and Liath's lives on my shoulders. I'm not Atlas, I can't take it." Said shoulders sink beneath the added weight. Any more and I'll be forever stooped. Might as well start calling me Hunchback.

Then Dylan does something completely out of character; he gets all up into my personal space, lays a heavy hand on my shoulder, looks me deep in the eyes; his stormy grey ones full of determination, mine flaring light blue with startled confusion, and says with no ounce of sway in his voice, "We're coming with." And he walks away, back to our falling apart family in the cafeteria.

Left speechless, mouth gaped open, brain fried, and tears prickling my eyes I admit to myself and only to myself how grateful I am that Annabelle and I don't have to tread through the muck alone. Even if them coming adds a possible burden – their potential demise – to my ever growing list.

Into my books, I fled.

Leaving those pesky

demons in my mind and

letting the characters

steal my heart.

Chapter 8

Back in the beautiful silence of my room I suppress the urge to go over in excruciating detail the events of the past few days. For me it would be torture replaying everything again and again and wondering what I could've done differently. The problem is that there is absolutely nothing I could've done. Had I gone out on my own the demon still would've found me and with my personality I would've told everyone and everyone included Annabelle. So we'd still be leaving. She wouldn't have gotten hurt, but still we would be leaving. We could've not gone at all, but eventually as I always did, I'd get cabin fever and abandon the sanctuary for a day of danger and violence. And if it was true that the demons were after me, they would've found me slaughtering their brothers. There was just no way around any of it. No matter what angle I looked, speculations I took, or events I contemplated, the end was inevitable and unchanging.

So no, I won't go over every agonizing detail of the past few days. I won't let myself remember the raw pain in Annabelle's voice as she screamed out to me. I won't let myself wonder what I could've done differently. Instead I turn to my newest obsession and one I staved off for as long as possible: Apocalypse myths.

At the beginning of all this I didn't allow myself to touch any book that might contain something about The End. Back then it didn't seem possible. Instead I obsessively studied. I finished school with what I would think are straight "A's". I worked on college-level homework and learned multiple languages. I did anything and everything to keep my mind off the impossible. But now, not only is it possible, it is the only answer left.

Within thirty minutes I am sitting cross legged on the floor, pencil tucked behind my ear, back hunched over, a sea of open books surrounding me. I am flitting from one page to the next, mind absorbing everything from the Norse apocalypse, Ragnorak, which basically ends the way the Christian mythology begins with only a man and a woman left to the Christian ending of water, but that's only if you think the Bible is a myth. There is also a myth that the world would end in fire. Thank you, Mayans. A lot of endings involved the ridding of sin – Egyptian, Christian, Judaism, and so many more. Most of the time the sin was disbelief. Whether it was the Egyptians denouncing Ra, the Sun God, or the Christians and Jewish not praying to God. And then there's the Babylonian apocalypse – the story of Utnapishtim – that strongly echoes the great flood in the Bible and the story of Noah, right down to the boat and the repopulating of the Earth. There are so many! Some ended in plagues, some in fire, so many in water, but none of them has anything to do what is going on now! Yes, almost all have demons somewhere in their mythology, but none are in conjunction with Armageddon.

It is hopeless.

Cara saunters in just then. I have never been so happy to see her face in my life.

"What's up?" I ask with honest cheer.

The cheer doesn't rub off on Cara. It never does. She drops a huge duffel bag at my feet and commands, "Pack."

"For?"

"You're leaving," she answers.

"Wow, you look so broken up about it," I quip sarcastically. Yes, it is my decision to leave, but she doesn't have to be so damn eager to get rid of me. I assumed Cara would miss me the least, but I hadn't expected her to all but shove me out the door.

Instead of throwing her lethal selection of sarcastic comments back at me, she says something that truly surprises and touches me, "The rest of us have already packed," then she has to add, "we're just waiting on you," in her usually bitchy manner. Ah, the Cara we know and love.

In that moment I don't do what a normal person would have and what I want to – leap up from where I sit, hug Cara, and profusely thank her for making the impending journey survivable. No, I calmly nod my head and say I'll pack.

For a while after she leaves I just sit there. We would survive. When it was only Belle and I going I knew it was a suicide mission. When it was us joined by Liath and Dylan we had a fifty-fifty chance. But with all of us going? There is no doubt we'll survive. On top of all that fantastic news, the guilt that attacked me like a predator after its prey has disappeared. I am no longer responsible for stealing the Brains and the Peacekeeper.

Letting out a sigh of relief, I get up to pack. This is only the first of many things to do. We'll need to pack a decent amount of food, guns, other weapons, and ammo. The vehicles will need to be serviced; tire pressure, oil level, and all that other good stuff. We'd also need a healthy supply of bandages and other first aid supplies. We never know what we'll run into and no matter how well we wield weapons, scrapes and bruises are unavoidable.

The checklist continues to grow in my head as I fold and place sensible clothes – jeans, cotton shirts, socks, underwear – into the duffel bag that lay at the foot of my soon to be abandoned bed. Not for the first time I wonder if we are making the right choice. We have a home here, no matter how unordinary. Everything we know resides in this school. Out there we are fish on land. We're settlers treading into uncharted territory. Wrong or right, I don't have a choice in the matter, so I move on with the checklist. A map. Not an ordinary one, but one that focuses on back streets. The highways will be too densely packed with abandoned vehicles and decaying bodies. On top of that pleasantness, we'll be much too far from whatever food we can scavenge and homes we can rest. With Annabelle injured, we would need to rest. No question about it.

Before I zip up the duffel bag full of my dressers contents, I carefully wrap the picture of my Papa, me and my Mama, my Mama's locket, my Papa's badge, the photos of Annabelle and I alone and the one with Mom and Dad, Dad's bible, and my mom's cross in an old, holey, pajama t-shirt and gingerly set the bundle on top of the folded clothes. On instinct I reach into my nightstand and grab the notebook that hides inside. With a couple of pencils I add it to my horde. I had a feeling written word might be one of my only outlets if we ever made it to civilization.

Duffel bag in hand I head toward the door. Glancing briefly at my wall of weapons a morbid thought hits me; I'll need another bag, a much bigger bag. I shake off the thought. I won't let myself get caught up in its sticky tendrils. We killed things, demons, and sometimes even people – only the soulless, deranged and dangerous – it's how we survived. Weapons are necessary. I like them. They make me feel safe.

In the empty halls, even my light footsteps echo. Though our home is normally quiet because of its massive size, now, today it is almost too quiet. No faint clicking of silverware on plates meets my ears. No hushed speaking is to be heard. No other footsteps vibrate down the halls. Fear of abandonment slices quickly through my heart. Suppressing the urge to run and shout out everyone's names, I calmly, briskly walk to the infirmary.

Annabelle is missing.

Now the need to run and shout becomes nearly overwhelming. I manage, however, to breathe in through my nose, out through my mouth and think logically. Cara had said they'd all packed. Where do you take packed bags? To the car. Parking lot it is.

Annabelle's ass better not be out there. My pace picks up. Despite the barbed wire and wall of decaying bodies, it isn't safe out there. Not really. The wall of dead's purpose was to repel the demons. That is all but the scavenger demons. It's a little known fact that all demons, aside from the scavenger type, despise corpses. Corpses are mere carcasses to them. Soulless, anger-less, hate-less, greed-less, useless. Basically devoid of all possible nutrients.

Now scavenger demons, they're different. Those bulbous eyed creatures with fur missing in some places, burnt in others, all jutted bones, broken claws, and chipped teeth take what they can get. Not only are they carnivores, but they're also notorious cannibals. That's why killing them where they're hunched over their already dead victims makes more sense them keeping them away with the others; Wraiths and Succubi and Soul Stealers and the Nightmares and all the other wicked things. One of us is almost always out there, shotgun in hand, guarding. The front door meets my palms before my mind catches up with my feet. Sure enough, Annabelle is sprawled across the steps, apple half way to her smiling lips.

My parental nature takes over before I can stop it, "What in the hell do you think you're doing!?" she flaps her lips silently as if to answer, but I barrel right over her feeble attempt, "You almost died yesterday. Do you know what that means?" she shakes her head, wheat blond tresses bouncing wildly, "It means you need to be resting."

Pointedly I ignore everyone's chill-out glances and wait for Annabelle to respond.

She fires back with attitude, "The key word in that statement is almost."

"What?" I ask, daring her to repeat herself.

She takes the dare, a glint of defiance in her pale blue eyes, "I *almost* died." Belle drags the word out for my benefit.

Had she not been injured I would've leapt across the landing, effectively closing the five feet of space between us, and rung her neck. But I don't. Calmly, I force myself to let loose my fingers and unclench my jaw. Liath, our biased peacekeeper where Belle is concerned, steps in then.

"Whoa, chill, Leila. She's only getting some air." His burly hands are up in a placating gesture. I want to punch him in the face. But I won't. Or so I tell myself. And I don't. Leila 2, Anger 0.

It won't solve anything anyway. What would solve something is calling in my own biased buddy. I run my tongue over my teeth and prepare to wipe that "I win" smirk off Annabelle's pretty face.

"Hey, Ezekiel!" I spot him by the SUV loading up what looks like food. Waving him over I add, "I could use your muscles."

He jogs over to me and I take a moment to admire his lithe frame. Ezekiel is one of those guys blessed with a muscular neck that flares out to toned shoulders and back. His biceps could choke me if he barely flexed. He has a chiseled chest. From his chest his waist tapers off into to-die-for abs. his legs are tree trunks; firm and immovable if that's what he wanted. Overall he is a spectacular sight.

Once in front of me he asks, "What can I do for you Blue Eyes?"

I smile, a rare, genuine one, and taunt, "Could you be more original?"

"Princess?"

I scrunch up my nose and shake my head. He appraises me. Starting at my face then down to my toes and back again. "Angel?"

Holding back the chuckle, I reply, "I'm pretty sure I crawled out of Hell, not fell from Heaven."

This time when his eyes wander up and down and over me, my insides crawl, but in a delicious way. "You certainly are Temptation in its finest from." He bites his lip unconsciously and I lock my knees together to keep from swooning.

I clear my throat to help bring me back to the moment and away from his hypnotic gaze. Seeming to notice this, Ezekiel smiles and asks, "So how can I help you Angel?" looks like the nickname stuck.

Gesturing towards Annabelle I say, "You could escort this one back to the infirmary."

"Bodyguard style or fireman?"

"Fireman."

Annabelle looks appalled and thoroughly defiant; it's apparent in the way she holds herself – chin out, shoulders back, hands on cocked hips. "You wouldn't dare."

"Wouldn't I?" I let my resolve seep through. Her defiant stance doesn't falter.

"Go for it." I tell Ezekiel and start toward the truck.

Out of the corner of my eye I catch Liath moving to intervene. One look and he is silenced. A squeal of surprise meets my ears and then "Put me down" and small fists hitting muscular back. No matter how she tried there was no way she'd make head way. Brute strength had never been her strong suit.

Amused I spin around to witness the spectacle. What I see – Annabelle slung like a doll over Ezekiel's broad shoulder, her face at his butt and her feeble kicks and wiggles in attempt to get back on solid ground – makes me giggle a giggle I long thought extinct.

One after another burst out of me as tears roll down my cheeks. I can't stop them. The way Annabelle futilely struggles and Ezekiel seems unfazed strikes a chord with me. Maybe it is just him though. Realizing I am right a blush creeps across my cheeks. Perhaps all the crazy up and down emotions stem, not only from Annabelle's accident, but also from Ezekiel's sudden appearance. It correlates.

Not having time to dissect this new theory and not really wanting to either I choose a distraction and an important one at that; our survival.

"What's been done?"

Rudy speaks up. "Truck, van, and your bike are serviced. Annabelle's was salvageable."

"Thank God. Give it to Ezekiel."

"Will do."

I incline my head. He continues. "We have freeze dried meals out the wazoo—"

"Did you just say wazoo?"

Rudy ignores me. "Ammunition is in a Rubber Maid in the back of the truck and van."

"Smart to have it in both."

Inclining his head in silent thanks he continues, "We have bags of rice and other dry foods like beans stacked in the truck. Cans and freeze dried fruits and veggies and what junk food that's still edible is in those," he points to large bins in the trunk of the mini van.

"And my bike?"

Dylan speaks up. "Tip top shape. The compartment is full of MRE's should we get separated. No ammo though."

Good choice. I prefer my knifes and crossbow. Virtually soundless and reusable.

He forges on. "Maps are in all vehicles. Back roads like you asked."

"Good."

"Clothes?" I ask.

"All packed bags are either going in the truck or the van. I don't know if you packed—"

"I have."

"Well good. And you packed?"

"Only what was necessary."

Knowing he wouldn't get any more details he moves on. "So, when are we leaving?"

"A day or two," I reply.

"Waiting for Annabelle to heal."

"As much as she can."

Dylan walks towards the fence. I follow. "She looks on the mend."

I can't argue. Annabelle this morning vs Annabelle last night is a startling difference. Positive startling. Her ghostly complexion returned to its usual pale pallor. The pink that spoke of life last night is brighter, more vivid. Especially when she gets angry. Like she did this morning. My lip twitches, wanting to grin. Her hair is done and shiny like usual. Had I not been there when she was bleeding her life's blood on a dirty mattress, I would've given her a clean bill of health.

"I'd still like to wait."

"And we will."

Watching the scavenger demons pick at the unidentifiable bodies, I reiterate, "There's no rush."

"Nope." He agrees again.

We stand there in comfortable silence for a while; both aware I can't stall much longer. The packing hadn't even taken a day. People – Cara mostly -- would be pushing to leave soon. Very soon. It surprises me that nobody else had reservations. They are all gung ho, packed, and ready. Almost like they planned it.

I won't allow my suspicious inner thoughts to go on any longer than the gang would let the silence. Liath steps up to my side, swings his arm over my shoulder; a gesture that is completely him, and says louder than necessary, "Did you really have to do that?"

I don't have to ask what he is talking about. Annabelle. He is always talking about Annabelle.

"Probably not."

"Had to prove a point."

Nudging him with my shoulder I answer, "You know me."

He nudges me back, almost tipping me over. His arm over my shoulder is the only thing that keeps me standing. "She's pouting."

"And?"

"And—"

"She'll get what she wants soon enough." If I can hear the irritation and resent in my voice so can he. But he lets it slide.

Removing his arm from my shoulder he starts to walk away. Pausing not two feet from me he says, "She wants to leave tomorrow."

The news strikes me like lightening. Understanding sizzles through my veins in place of electricity. Instead of hair standing on end eyes open wide. She could do that. I owe her. "She's not in charge." It is a feeble attempt to calm myself. It doesn't work.

"Neither are you." Peacekeeper, my ass.

Then he walks away like it is nothing. Like confirming my fears is nothing. Belle can dictate when we leave. She already invoked part of the agreement. We are leaving. No questions asked. But the other part is deciding when. Like I did.

Ugh. How had I overlooked this one small, humongous detail?

"She's not in charge." Dylan tries to soothe my worries.

We both know he is wrong. That I am wrong.

I squeak out, "Is there anything left to pack?"

The remorse in his voice threatens to buckle my knees. "No."

With that he leaves me to yet another on-verge panic attack. Annabelle is going to kill me. Feeling the rusted metal chain-link fence bite into the tender flesh of my palm I collapse against its sturdy frame. The scavengers pop up their heads at the noise but quickly dismiss me. Apparently, I'm not dead enough for them. At least not visibly.

If I was being honest, at least with myself, there are a handful of reasons I absolutely don't want to leave. First and foremost among the bunch; I am afraid. For so many reasons – Annabelle's accident, the unknown, our survival rate, but most of all, I am deathly afraid of the Biologicals. For the gang I'd walk right up to their doorstep and beg for help, but I don't want to. Their help is the last thing I want. From them the only thing I ever wanted was an explanation. Why wasn't I good enough? Long ago I squashed the notion. I'd thrown out everything pertaining to them, but Belle, trying to help, refused me that right.

It isn't fair what she is asking of me. Part of me resents her for that, but her reasoning is pure: my safety. If only she knew that the Biological's is the most dangerous place for me. Right now, I'm in a fairly decent place. They would ruin that. But for her, like I'd done so many other things and given up so much, I'd grovel if it meant my family got a warm meal and a safe place to sleep. Yep, I certainly am the loose cannon, but that isn't all the Fate's had in store for me. I am also prone to sacrifice.

All I could do was

breathe and tell myself

I'd survive this like

everything else.

Chapter 9

Walking up to Belle's door I read the first sign of her rebellious nature, no joke it is an actual sign: F*CK OFF!. The girl is too much. Usually I'd waltz right in, but the door knob looks dangerous and uninviting in this moment or maybe that's how I picture Annabelle, so I settle for knocking.

"Who is it?"

Wish she would've opened the door first. Now there is like a zero percent chance that she'll let me in.

"Leila."

"Go away."

I am right. Surprise, surprise.

"No."

And stubborn.

"I don't want to talk to you."

"I know."

"Then why are you here?" she asks.

"Because I want to talk to you."

Her involuntary groan of irritation is evidence that she is giving in. I am far more stubborn than her and annoying if I choose to be and she knows it.

One minute passes. 56. 57. 58. 59. Two minutes. After ten minutes I still remain rooted in the same place. Another thirty seconds and I begin to hear rustling. The sound lasts for a few moments before it stops. I wait another few minutes and finally the knob turns.

I am met by a choice gesture and a disgruntled face. "Traitor."

Okay, so she is really pissed.

And I am about to make it worse, "Calm down." At least for a bit.

"Calm down!" her face contorts into a look of absolute disbelief, "You had a guy throw me over his shoulder and cart me off to my room. And then," she throws her hands up indicating there is more, "then he drops me off in my room like I am a child."

Finished she crosses her arms over her chest and waits. Probably for an apology. She won't be getting one. "You were acting like one."

"And you," she points an accusing finger my way, "are acting like a dictator."

I let the comment roll off me like water on metal and continue to be diplomatic, "I'm not here to fight with you."

"Then leave." Belle practically growls. I wouldn't be surprised to see spittle fly off her pulled back lips.

I sigh a sigh of exhaustion. I hate when she is like this; stubbornly defiant…just like me. "Would you please hear me out?"

"Why?"

"Because it's in your best interest." I don't like this. Not one bit. But better to not be blindsided.

"How so?" She is a suspicious little one.

Here goes. "It's your choice when we leave."

"We have to finish packing."

"Done."

"Vehicles –"

"—Done."

"So?"

"We can leave whenever." I answer her unspoken question.

Ignoring my comment, she asks, "Don't want to be caught off guard?" She knows me. Too well.

I ignore her in turn. "So, boss woman, when we leaving?"

In the following moment we both hold our breathe. Me, because I hope desperately that given the authority to decide when we leave will scare her into staying. Her, probably because she is scared and was debating whether or not to back down. We both know the inevitable outcome.

"Tomorrow."

Having nothing to say I slide my right foot behind me, leaving it poised on the ball and pivot. As if Death himself is riding the winds behind me, I flee from the doom Annabelle bound us to. She doesn't follow.

When she looked behind her

all she saw was the

gaping abyss

that separated her

from all she used to be.

Chapter 10

The red-ish pink that speaks of morning dances its way across the sky. The moon fades. For now. Shafts of light penetrate the bare windows. With no shades to block it, it assaults the eyes. Begrudgingly I open them. Morning. Today feels no different than any other, but it is.

No longer are there constant reminders of the ordeal two nights ago. The wounds on my arm and face have healed incredibly well. I'm left with virtually no scar tissue. What is there will fade with time. Evidence of the assault on myself has vanished too. Every reason for our departure fled, and with it my bravery.

What I want is to sink back in bed, close my eyes and pretend today isn't the day all ends – safety, security, normalcy or what passes for it—but I can't. I must face the dawn. My people need me. Reluctantly, I squirm out of the fortress of pillows and blankets. Inching to the edge of the bed, swinging my legs over the side, stopping to feel the thick white carpet find its way between my toes; all methods of delaying what will happen anyway. The shag rug; an improvement to the generic patterned carpet the school put it. Ugly green. Ugly purple. Ugh, checks. I'm going to miss its softness caressing me as I laid down to read.

Sitting for a while longer I continue to prolong every moment. The minute I actually merge my feet with the floor is the end. My eyes wander, examining every inch of the room – two short mahogany dressers, two mismatched antique looking night stands, two lamps; one generic black pole and white shade, the other with six swivel heads in the colors of the rainbow, sturdy oak bed frame and comfortable mattress. Whoever finds this place, if someone does, will be living comfy.

The night before we locked down the fortress. Any other possible entrances secured, gates fortified, food locked away. No demons would be getting in. The last touch would be to chain and padlock the front doors. Humans would find a way in, but hellions wouldn't bother.

Feet shuffling of their own accord, the *swish swish* of beaded curtain comes before anticipated. The familiar swiftly blurs past. It's not like in the movies where goodbye is a moment to remember. Home could never be forgotten. Blue double doors rush up; the last barrier. I push through, for a moment saying no to hesitation.

Harsh light momentarily impairs my vision. I'm left to squint in order to grasp my surroundings. Blurry shapes take form. One presents itself as obviously human. The rest must be in the nearby vehicles.

Nonchalantly, I ask, "Been waiting awhile?"

He shrugs his massive shoulders in response. "Annabelle wanted to wake you a while ago. Told her to wait."

"Thanks."

Again he shrugs. Rudy's never liked praise or gratitude. It's always made him sort of uncomfortable. "Did you want to shower?"

"Nah, I'm good," I reply.

"Sure? Everyone else did and it could be a bit."

"Yeah, but I showered last night and I'm not all that worried."

"Why's that?"

Though he asked, we answer in tandem. "Dylan."

That boy could work wonders.

The easy going moment subsides. Its end brought on by the appearance of chains and a padlock in Rudy's outstretched hand. They'd likely been there the whole time and I was either too tired to notice or my subconscious understanding their meaning blocked them out. Either way it is time to face them and what they mean.

"Care to do the honors?"

It's my turn to shrug. "Why the hell not?"

Rudy passes me the chains, which I slide through the handles of the doors. Next comes the padlock. I click it into place. Only afterwards asking, "What's the pass code?"

"2023." The year we left. Clever. None of us would forget that.

The year makes me think of the month and in turn the date. I shake my head.

"What?"

"A month from Christmas and we're homeless."

He looks stricken. "Seriously, it's the 25th?"

"Yes."

"Time flies..."

"When it doesn't matter," I finish.

Without another word I bound the steps two at a time and hop on my bike. Pre-routed destination in mind I rev the engine and take off. I don't look back for one more glimpse of the home I'm leaving. I don't even look back to make sure they're following. I just fly. For two hours straight I fly; swerving around wrecked cars and building debris, avoiding discarded goods and the littered bones of the Fallen. I don't worry about how the groups making it through the patch work of obstacles. Four wheel drive's amazing. I try not to worry about what we will do once we get where we're going. And once I reach a straight patch of untouched road I kick it up a notch. The wind in my face, the yellow lines of the road blurring beneath my tires is exhilarating. I enjoy every second. Only to stop when they call. It's time to stop. Bathroom break.

Coming down from my high I lose the smile I'd won back. I have to back track to the rendezvous point --a tiny little mom and pop gas station. While the miscreants; that's what I'm referring to them as of right now, eagerly await their chance at the bathroom and Dylan does his magic and pumps what little gas is left into each of the three vehicles -- truck, van, both motorcycles -- respectively, I head in search of food. Doing the mundane task allows my mind to wander.

I've said not a single word to any of them. I guess in my own way I blame them. They should've put up a fight. Argued that Annabelle and I were insane. They most certainly shouldn't have packed up and left with us willingly. No doubt, I'm totally glad they're here, but I'd rather be grumpy with them back there. And then on top of that they drag me back here with them...the traitors...to pee and eat. I could've easily done that on my own. Would've preferred it.

Throughout my enteral rant I'm gathering food. Most people don't stop to think of the long term. They'll ransack the chips and bread and peanut butter and jelly.

The meats and fruits and other perishables. Canned food is discarded. Actually not even that, they just waltz right past it, probably thinking what good is it without a can opener. It's plenty good and we so happen to have the nifty tool. The basket I grabbed on my way over to the canned food section is filled to the brim with soups of all varieties, green beans and corn, pineapple and peaches, beans and even canned meat. We hit the mother load. One more day we could leave our travel stock pile alone. Better to scavenge and eat what we can find. When we are desperate we'll loot the bins, but for now canned food will do. And apparently jerky...Cara was smart enough to check the manager's office.

After divvying up the food we take a moment to rest and eat. Conversation bounces back and forth among the miscreants. I remain stoic and silent. I've nothing to say to them. Not right now. Not when I'm angry beyond compare. At them. At the situation. At the whole world. I don't want to go grovel for help from the people who threw me away. I don't want their food or their money or their guidance. I'm teeming with bitterness. It's staining my insides and turning into hate. More fuel for the beast.

After relieving myself I'm ready to straddle my bike for another two hours.

Liath chooses now to intervene. "What gives?"

I look at him questioningly.

"You haven't said a single word to any of us. Haven't even checked in on Annabelle."

"Seriously! That's what this is about? Your precious little girlfriend." He's eyes widen at the malice in my tone. A sign of surprise. Well I'm not done yet. "That girlfriend of yours is the reason we're even out here scavenging for food and careening towards what could very well be our deaths. Not to mention my certain mental break down." Okay, so I held a little resentment towards my sister. Could anyone really blame me? Of all the things I'd made her do because of my gut instincts, none of them involved her abusive father or bystander mother. None. But she has the audacity to make me encounter my worst nightmare!

During my rant Liath's been defending her. Anger sizzles through my veins and places bile on my tongue. I lash out with venom, "Leave me alone and go scamper back to the cripple."

Liath visibly cowers back as if I've struck him. His mouth gapes open as he tries to form words.

Not wanting to wait around and hear them, I swing my right leg up and over the seat and settle in for a long ride.

Within four and a half hours of riding and stopping only to pee and fuel myself and the motorcycle, I check in once. I refuse to stop with them until it's time to find a place to bunker down for the night. We knew it'd be necessary. We were aware that with Annabelle injured and demons lurking we couldn't and shouldn't travel without at least the dim rays of sunlight that filtered in despite the smokes attempts to eradicate the light. Even this far away from the epicenter the unclear air clogs the nose and assaults the eyes.

Veering off path I locate the least disturbed house in the neighborhood. It's a two story and while I wouldn't usually go for that, simply because the lack of escape routes on the top floor, it's the best option for the size of our group. Too many people in too crammed of space leaves little room to maneuver and defend if necessary. Also, the miscreants are probably exhausted and need rest. The two story looks more likely to have more beds then the surrounding single stories. That in mind, I radio in my location and seek to clear the house. Room after room proves empty. By the time I've finished the miscreants have arrived.

Rudy's quick to lecture me about the dangers of clearing a house alone. "There could've been demons," but there wasn't and he knows that. How? I wasn't disposing bodies when they got here. "If not demons, then Deranged or Souless." Both are dangerous. But I already knew that. He continued to go on like that; face slightly red…getting redder with each moment I don't speak, hands gesturing wildly. Rudy is losing his temper. A rare sight. He is normally very composed.

His change in demeanor fails in eliciting any response from me. I don't bother to pretend to listen. Had I had gum I would've been smacking noisily and blowing bubbles. But since that is a rare commodity, everything is a commodity in the After, that eludes me, I just stare off into space.

Unable to take any more of my "games" as he calls them, Rudy stalks off. The first time I've seen him stalk off without a target. Probably because I am the target.

Shimmying off the slimy coating of guilt, I stalk away as well and leave everyone to bicker about the bathroom schedule while I focus on more important tasks. Since this isn't a long term camp-out I can only barricade so much. The house must have only one outside access point; to make for easy guarding, and two inside exit points for easy escape. The sliding glass door isn't optimum, but it's what I have to work with.

After a moment of debate I decide a leg from the table. It'll make a great wooden bar substitute and can only be removed from the inside. Having already rendered the table useless, I employ the last three legs to bar the downstairs windows. The upstairs windows are left as they are – locked – and checked and double checked. Unless a winged demon manages to discern movement through the shut blinds, we are safe.

Done with that I open my mouth for the first time in hours. "Mackenzie you've showered?"

Not one to hold a grudge, she answers, "Yes."

"Take the rice from the cupboard and cook it. Also, boil water for drinking." As an afterthought I add please. She's not the one to blame anyway. Her passive attitude wouldn't have allowed her to intervene. Without hesitation she leaves to do what's asked of her.

Looking for crimson locks I spot them easily. "Liath!" He's just as loyal as Kenzie and waits for instruction, "The cans of beans need to be divvyed up."

"Done." He shoots me a shy smile over his shoulder as he leaves. Not only does the boy forgive me for my outburst but is worried I don't forgive him. I manage my lips into a semblance of a smile. No matter my mood, he didn't deserve what I dished.

Still I don't feel like talking. There is a well of venom in my stomach waiting to find the right time to slither up my throat and strike in the form of words. Bypassing any attempts at conversation, I head up the stairs. Time to scavenge.

The house obviously had been home to teenage girls. If the two girly bedrooms full of scattered clothing and make-up wasn't enough of a clue then their stockpile of razors and tampons were. I stole a bit of each. There are some commodities I refuse to live without. Toothbrush graces the top of the list. Toothpaste a close second. Finding both these items in the hall closet, I grab one of each. I'd brought my own, but more never hurt.

Continuing my search of the hall closet I find bubble bath. Mhmm and it's a beachy scent. Sea salt and sand. I know what I'm doing when it's my turn in the bathroom; soaking. As I confiscate the bubble bath a door opens. The faint click of automatic unlock reaching my ears and letting me know its bath time.

Undressed, I sit in the porcelain tub, cool against my back as steaming, bubbly water rises. As soon as the bubbles coat my entire body, I turn the water off with a flick of my ankle. The scent of the steam wafting beneath my nose and the dark of the unlit bathroom soothing my dirt tinged eyes lulls me to sleep. I sink beneath the surface; a thought rises up, one I haven't thought in what feels like decades; my not-so-sweet sixteen. In the state I'm in, somewhere between consciousness and oblivion, bits and pieces of the event then somehow, someway, appear connected to the now. The one issue? I can't for the life of me decipher the puzzle I've created.

I retreated into myself

for once enjoying the labyrinth

that was my soul

--reveling in the chaos

that pervaded every inch of it:

A rarity.

Seeking out the darkest corner

I merged with the shadows

urging the past to steal me

away from the present.

Chapter 11

The usual faint light I'm accustomed to waking up to is replaced by a sun high in the sky. I've over slept. Or rather Belle didn't hop on my prone form and insist on waking me up with an off-key -- *severely* off-key -- Happy Birthday. Odd.

Even though the air smells of peanut butter, syrup, pancakes and bacon, the works for my favorite breakfast, the aroma isn't strong. Even the bitter scent of black coffee is fading. Something's wrong.

Not wanting to dwell on the unexplained and ruin a very special day, I skip down the stairs, a bright smile plastered on my face in case someone's waiting. But there's no one. My cheerful skip falters and my face falls when I see the note on the refrigerator door.

Dad's at work. Emergency on site Belle and I out shopping.

Breakfast in fridge. See you for dinner!

Happy Birthday, sweetie. I love you!!!

xoxo

Mom

Ripping the note from the fridge, I shred it, toss it, and go about re-heating my birthday breakfast. By the time I'm done eating and the dishes are done everyone's still gone. Trying my best to not let their absence ruin the day I go to my room and call the girls; Pinky and Elvira. Both say they'll be over in thirty. Just enough time to get ready.

In the bathroom the toothbrush is half way to my mouth when I freeze and it clatters in the sink below. Minty green paints an abstract picture in the bowl, but I hardly notice. I'm too preoccupied with the "new" me. Crazy as it may sound I look entirely different. Before I went to bed last night everything about me was soft, subdued and just pretty. I was only a girl. The morning me screamed WOMAN!!!

Instinctively my hands go to my face and frantically rub. Despite some redness, nothing returns to the way it should. My cheekbones remain dangerously sharp, like a razor's edge, with a hint of blush marking them as still oddly welcoming. My nose appears more prominent. Jaw stronger, yet with a delicate air. Hair darker. Thicker. Longer. Curlier, but in an untamable, animalistic sort of way. Eyelashes mirror hair in the sense that their darker, thicker, longer. Like I'd fly away with a stiff wind. If that were possible.

Even my lips are different; fuller and pouting of their own accord. And my eyes. Just wow. They are astonishing. Bluer than I'd ever seen them. And not just one blue. They flickered from the palest blue in the sky to the darkest in the sea. If that weren't enough, even my body had made the shift towards womanly.

My breasts had magically outgrown my bra by what appeared to be two cup sizes. Stomach flattened, waist narrowed, hips flared. I was a Coke bottle. Overnight I morphed from the picture of innocence to Aphrodite.

But that isn't possible. Years' worth of physical changes just isn't possible. I am seeing things. I have to be.

Getting dressed is a pain. Nothing fits right. Too tight in newly developed places, too loose in others. Frustrated and beyond annoyed, I settled for a skirt that manages to cling to my waist and one of Annabelle's half shirts. I may not be fit to walk a run way; mall, yes.

Bypassing the front door I slip out of the back. Not bothering with the locks, I spot my blue and neon green cruiser by the rickety old shed where I left it, wheel it out through the side gate and into the front. The girls – one flaming red hair, the other sleek black – wait at the end of the drive way, their bikes relaxing on kickstands.

Once I reach them I'm met with curiosity swimming in bright green and rich chocolate eyes. So I'm not crazy. I'm not sure whether I should be relieved or concerned. More than likely seeing the confusion in my twin blue pools, Elvira makes light of the situation.

"If this is what happens at sixteen, I can't wait!"

Pinky joins in, "I know right! Like wow, curves." She makes a gesture with her hands countless guys have displayed at the other more womanly girls.

All three of us crack up. Unladylike laughter peeling out of us in waves. By the time we compose ourselves there are tears streaming down our flushed faces and we're clutching our sore stomachs. Suddenly my day's better.

Fair skinned Pinky hops on her, what do you know, hot pink bike with its black basket on the front and caramel complexion. Elvira gets on her orange and white flowered bike. Her basket's also white with real flowers running through the wicker. The girl has a green thumb.

Following their lead, I swing my leg over my bike and plop onto the comfy seat. I have a basket too, actually two; so do the girls, one in the front and one in the back, except mine's made from shipping crates. Dad has a way with tools.

After our trip, all six baskets are bound to be filled to the brim with various clothes, shoes, and accessories. Birthdays were for shopping or so we decided. It's a good thing we all had jobs. The mall was our playground, our safe place. It's where we could be stupid and mess around. Where we could try on expensive clothes we'd never be able to afford. It was sophomore year.

Back at the house, we again disregard the front door and as a group file in through the well sanded gate, as Dad always points out. "You won't get a splinter from my gates." I can hear him boasting in my head. I'd missed him at breakfast. A lot.

This is the first year I'd been allowed to invite anyone over for my birthday dinner. Again I get to choose one of my favorites: spaghetti and meat sauce. Mmm. And Mom makes it extra special with a secret ingredient -- cinnamon. Can't wait! That is if they even bother to show up. Maybe my friends were allowed because they wouldn't be coming.

That thought forefront, I pull open the back door and ... SURPRISE!!! A rainbow of confetti gets thrown at me. A party horn goes off somewhere, maybe here or there. Blue and green streamers distract the eye. Red and purple balloons join the party.

People. There are people everywhere. Stupid multi-colored hats strapped under their chins. Some are polka dotted. Others striped. I'm bombarded by a sea of hands and arms and "*happy birthdays*" and "*wow sixteen already*". I lose track of how many hugs I give. Throughout it all I feel terrible. I shouldn't have doubted my family. They've gone above and beyond. My first birthday party since Mama and Papa. Tears sting the eyes, but embarrassment isn't in the cards, so suppressed I turn to the crowd and say loud enough to reach every corner of the house, "Thank you!" And the party begins.

But first, before I can join, Elvira and Pinky drag me upstairs to change. Shopping for dresses doesn't seem so random now. Together we change: Pinky in an emerald green, crochet back, floor length piece that's just perfect for a slightly fancier than casual gathering; Elvira in a peach high-low dress that compliments her gardening forged calves; and me in a simple red, tighter than I'm used to, mid-thigh sweater dress with long sleeves. Our shoes go beautifully with not only our dresses but our personalities too: Pinky in fancy brown and gold encrusted gladiator sandals; Elvira in simple, practical teal flats; me in black, tattered Converse. Ready, we head down the hall, a night of fun and delicious food on our minds.

I distinctly remember the beginning of the party being normal. Fun even. Obviously, as was to be expected, I got odd stares, but unexpected: none from my mom, dad, or sister. But still things went on as normal. We ate and laughed and listened to music. Mixed and mingled with people other than my best friends. Annabelle is nowhere to be seen, which isn't odd because she hardly is present anymore. It isn't until karaoke gets kicking that things get strange.

Predictably I am pushed and prodded toward the stage or rather cleared out living room space by the television. Being a good sport I choose one of my favorite songs, "Let it Go" and sing. Perfection isn't expected. I have a terrible voice except when in the shower. Then I am a rock star. My family would disagree. But up there, on that "stage," I sounded just like Elsa. My voice was melodic, in tune and soulful. Those who really knew me looked surprised. Those who didn't looked thrilled. The first good singer of the night and it is the birthday girl.

After me some guy from my first period chemistry class did a horrible rendition of "Kiss the Girl". That wasn't the only horrible part...he sang it right at me. And not in a goofy it's your birthday sort of way. Worse than that, I was pretty sure he had a girlfriend.

I didn't realize until later, much later, that the moment I sang was the moment things really started to change. After that I was noticed: by boys who were single, those who weren't, men married and otherwise.

It's like my voice had triggered some invisible switch and I didn't know how to turn it back off.

The first of many incidents was by far the worst. Not because I was concerned. Not because I couldn't handle myself. I could. Papa's buddies made sure of that. It was the worst because the guy's girl caught him and blamed me. She made a scene at my party! It was humiliating and she was supposed to be my friend.

From that incident on I was marked as a leper. Not a single girl but Elvira and Pinky would go near me. Boys often came too close, way too close. They'd try to pull me towards them or grab my face so they could stare into my deep blue eyes as if they were in need of a high and the blue pools were the drug.

It was horrible. Hoodies and shades became my best friends. Nothing figure flattering was allowed. No colors. I wanted to fade into the background. And I did.

Weeks later, the horrible ordeal stayed with me. At night I was assaulted again and again. His clumsy hands would find me in the dark; pulling and tearing. My eyes would start watering as his cheesy tinged breathe met my nose. He'd come in for the kill and....

⟊ ⟊ ⟊ ⟊ ⟊

Hands grip arms and haul dead weight out of frigid water. The chill substance splashes over the sides and soaks everything below. A body, me, is lain down on a warm, dry surface. Two hands: dainty but firm, one on top of the other, continually press on my chest. They're going to break a rib if I don't stop them, but words stick to my mouth like peanut butter in a dogs. Moving on to option B: arms flail wildly. Hands stop. A frantic face peers down at me. Dark brown hair curtains around us, providing privacy. It's in this privacy that I see the raw fear and worry fighting against control in mocha and caramel streaked eyes. Cara. And she's crying.

Somehow the picture of the broken bitch, and I say that endearingly, allows me to speak. "What happened?" It comes out more frog than I'd wanted but they're words none the less.

"You tell me." Worry and fear effectively turn her back into the bitch I know and love.

"I don't know. I was taking a bath and…" The water was freezing. How long had I been in here? Had I fallen asleep?

"And I must've passed out. It was a long day." I finish. More to convince myself than her.

"Leila, you were under the water."

Okay, now she was just being plain stupid. "Duh. I was taking a bath."

"No. I mean you were completely submerged." She gestures a forceful pushing down motion with her hands, "head and all."

"So?"

"You've been in here for an hour and a half."

An hour and a half. There's no way. Nobody could survive that long. No human anyway. Like a stalker I latch on to the possibility and don't let go. "I could've just fallen asleep."

Cara doesn't look like she shares the same beliefs as me and quickly discounts my attempts at sanity. "We've all knocked on the door. You didn't answer, call out.

Nothing. We thought you were ignoring us, but I started to worry --"

"That proves nothing."

"--you were laying there death still. No bubbles. Blue lips. They still are you know."

"What?"

"Your lips, they're still blue."

I'm hesitant to confirm or deny her claims. The mirrors three feet away but I can't make myself get up. Eventually, I'll have to face the truth. Cara isn't lying. I know this, but to actually get up on shaky legs, make my way to the water slicked mirror and stare irrefutable proof in the eyes seems too difficult. Now or later. That's what it boils down to. Now it is. I can't prolong the inevitable. I've always been the get it over with type of person. Bad news? Give it to me first.

On Jell-O legs I stand. Gradually, as I take my first and second step, bones appear. When the mirror comes into view I turn to ice. Any warmth that might've seeped into my body drains out. I'm a ghost: so pale I'm transparent, blood shot eyes and blue lips. My hands are so wrinkled you'd think I was eighty. If it weren't for the ice in my veins I'd collapse.

"How?" The question comes out as a meek whisper.

Cara's answer is just as quiet, blending in with the rest of the silence. "I don't know."

The first instinct that arises is to beg Cara to keep this a secret. I turn to her ready to do just that but the spooked look of her tells me she isn't eager to tell the others.

I ask one question. "Between us?"

"Absolutely."

In the span of five minutes Cara and I become closer than we did in the last year. We're comrades now. Bound by the same secret. And secrets? They're a contract not even blood can void.

Hours later everyone's asleep and I'm sitting in a chair, cross bow in my lap, watching the door. As to be expected all the "couples" official and in the closet, as I like to say, are in respective bedrooms upstairs. Ezekiel's stuck on the couch. Near me. Great.

And he's not sleeping either. Instead he feels like chatting. Night watch isn't meant for chatting. He strongly disagrees. "So what was your problem today."

"Excuse me?" There's a clear warning in my voice.

He chooses to dismiss it. "You ignored everyone all day."

Well wasn't he observant. "And?"

"How come?"

"You like questions don't you?"

"Answers are better."

"Wasn't in the mood to talk."

He's insistent. "But why? Did you not want to leave?" And smart.

"It's complicated."

"I've got time."

I need to shut this down. Now. "Actually you don't. You need to sleep while you can."

"What about you?"

"I'm good."

Ezekicl's face shuts down for a second. There's absolute no expression whatsoever. I suppose this is what dumbstruck looks like. I'm unsure what I've said to create such a reaction, but I take the brief reprieve. It lasts much longer than I'd expect.

About an hour passes and I assume he's sleeping. His breathing is even. Nice and slow. And his mouth isn't moving.

It's the mouth not moving part that allows me to relax and fill the silence with my thoughts. Breathing under water combined with my blast from the past leaves me with way more questions than answers. Can someone be more than just human? Is it possible for demons to procreate with humans? Wouldn't there be some condition -- pre or post -- that prevents the zygote from forming. And even if it was possible there weren't demons back when sperm met egg and created me. Or was there?

I mean seriously, after everything I've seen I couldn't discount anything. For all I know I could be part Siren. It would explain a lot; me singing – Sirens are known for their entrancing voices -- and then my life changing, randomly waking up as a woman, my breathing under water: if that's what I did. The blue lips makes it debatable. But if I was half human and half Siren, then maybe.

But who knew? Not me. But there were two people who would know. Two people I swore to never ask anything of. Well, I was breaking that oath for Annabelle, might as well add in a couple questions for myself. Looks like this god awful trip wouldn't be a waste after all.

When you looked into my eyes

It wasn't like you saw my soul

--nothing so simple as that.

Rather you plunged your hand

into my chest and dispelled

the darkness that lived there for years.

With a singular stare you returned

my ability to feel.

And how frightening those emotions

were, because they were all

for you.

Chapter 12

Sometime during the night I wake up, which is my first trigger, on the couch, my second. No one's next to me which is a relief, but why I'm here puzzles me. A quick check of the surroundings provides the answer: Ezekiel decided he'd be night watch. Like he tends to do I find, he has me torn between quick to form anger and a lesser, but equally as strong, lighter feeling. I think it's happy surprise or gratitude. Positive emotions and I have a fickle relationship. They don't stay around long enough lately for me to easily identify them.

The rest, I find, was much needed. I feel rejuvenated and ready for another eight hours of riding. The lighter, warmer feeling spurs my words, "Thank you."

The silence now punctured, Ezekiel turns to find me awake. "Welcome."

"Your turn?" It's only fair I offer.

He shakes his head. Brown locks fly back and forth in an endearing way. You can't not watch. It turns him suddenly boyish for a moment. It's cute.

"Up for conversation?" I'm shocked by my own words. Imagining what's going on in his mind is difficult.

"Sure." Shock doesn't register in his expression nor his tone and I'm grateful. The gang would never know how lonely I am. They're too busy with their counterparts. In a group of seven with an almost equal ratio of boys to girls someone's bound to be left out. I was that person. Honestly, how much I craved human attention escaped me until number eight showed up and happened to be a very very attractive male.

But that's not the only thing that's drawing me to him. He's the only one that's challenged me in years. Even since the Before. He's witty and funny and to the point. I like it as much as I hate it. His intelligence is refreshing and his ornery attitude is both humorous and annoying. That he calls me out on my shit is surprisingly appealing.

At this point I know the way of the conversations on me. Ball's in my court, so to speak. But I'm unsure of what to say. My life is one dominated by violence and destruction of all sorts -- mind, body, soul-- and I feel those topics are better left alone. Added to those topics are those that could lead to flirting. I don't want to seem too interested. It's not safe to get close when there's a chance we won't all make it. The others are too far in, but me, I'm a fortress of stone and spikes and anger.

Him. Talking about him is the safest option.

"So how'd you get caught up in the apocalypse?"

"Choices."

Cryptic much. And I say so. I find it's easy to fall into the rhythm of playful banter with him. Natural even.

He laughs a soul lightening laugh. It's as if just that sound can absolve one of their many sins. And me, I have more than my fair share. "I didn't mean to be. It's a loaded question that requires a story."

His eyes gleam in anticipation. He wants to share and I find I want him to. So I push him. "I'm not going anywhere."

Ezekiel lunches into a tale of two young boys forged into brothers by the indecencies of life. I hadn't known that Rudy had followed someone into the army. The knowledge gleans insight into Ezekiel. He's twenty.

The brutality they meet on the street pales in comparison to those they find in war. They thought they were prepared, that escape was the right option, they were wrong. We, as people, haven't learned much from our ancestors. Violence is seen as a solution and not a cause. Ezekiel's hate of this fact mars his features and for the first time I see him as battle weary as the rest of us. His shoulders sag under the immense weight of the memory of pain and blood and death. Frown and furrow lines etch into his otherwise statuesque face. The only part of him that does not dim or sag is his eyes. They burn with a fury I wouldn't have pegged him capable of. It's there for a flash, but I don't mistake the animalistic nature that drove him for a moment. I add it to my list of what I know about him.

I move him forward with a question. "So why here?"

"I woke up one day and Rudy was gone. Just gone. There was no trace of him."

I knew this side of the story. Rudy heard what was going on over here and abandoned the army in attempts to rescue

Cara. While that didn't work out quite as planned, there's no denying we wouldn't all be alive without him.

Ezekiel continues, a haunted look in his bright green eyes. "No one knew where he was. Most didn't care. Assumed he was a deserter. At the time the war was bad, so bad. We were losing people left and right. It was absolute chaos."

"That sounds terrible."

"It was," he murmurs. He's lost for a moment. I see the memories flashing before him, drawing him in. Visibly, he shakes himself, "Anyways with no place to start there was nothing I could do. Weeks passed before I saw what changed everything."

It changed everything for me too: that news broadcast. He didn't see the by-the-minute one that not only detailed the destruction but showed it in action. No, he got a recap. Not nearly as bad, but it brought him here, to me. Or rather Rudy.

He goes into pointless detail about the military's reaction to the disaster. Despite the images plastered across every television screen, newspaper and magazine they still believed it to be an act of terror.

Apparently that's why help took so long. People will believe what they want. They'll deny their very eyes and blame it on fatigue. Demons? They're things of story books. Even faced with them society represses the truth.

I try not to look bored but I can't hide it for much longer so I steer him towards the information I want to know, "So how'd you find us?"

Ezekiel takes the not so concealed hint and gives me an apologetic look. "After I figured out what the idiot was up to I got a friend to do aerial sweeps of San Jose--"

"But the smoke. How'd you see?"

"We weren't looking exactly."

"Exactly?"

"Our search was focused on the use of electronic devices." He looks proud of himself. "Eventually, we got a hit and I came down and starting searching."

I still didn't make sense to me. How could he possible find him. How? It's like a needle in a hay stack. I really big, really scattered hay stack.

Somehow reading my mind he answers the question before I can ask it. "Back in the war we'd developed a system of navigation. In case one of us got lost. N for north. W for west. S for south. E for east. A combination to indicate a mixed direction. Numbers stood for longitude and latitude. Each message would lead us to the next point. That's how I found you guys."

"But how'd you get to us before Rudy?" Curiosity and unlike the cat I didn't have nine lives. Too many questions and not enough answers. It is frustrating.

"I didn't. I made it to base right as Rudy was leaving. I accompanied him. He sent me to calm you while he focused on Belle. Then you started making a ruckus."

Oh. It made more sense now. Looking back Ezekiel had never made a move to hurt me. He was gentle even. Suddenly I feel silly. Why did I react like that?

I try and hide my embarrassment with more questions. "So what was your plan after you found Rudy?"

He doesn't hesitate. "I didn't have one."

I scoff. "So you just decided to waltz into a death zone with no plan of getting to safety?" No one's that selfless.

"I didn't waltz. I dropped down from a ladder." He states like it's no big deal. Maybe he was that selfless. Maybe Rudy did mean that much to him. But there's a nagging in my mind that tells me Rudy's not the only reason he blindly walked into danger. He's just that guy. Not a martyr but a savior. A useful addition to our band of misfits.

It's not my choice when we move off the topic. It's his, and he makes it perfectly clear he's done story telling. "And you know the rest."

"Yup." And conversation over. However; the silence isn't awkward. We are both lost in our own thoughts and it's peaceful.

Eventually, as all things do, this too ends. For a moment I hate myself for the traitorous feeling of disappointment that lurks deep within the recesses of my heart. I can't afford to care, let alone like somebody. The fact that all the others got under my skin irks me, but at least they've proven their will to live. I don't fear for them the way many would. The band of misfits can handle themselves. Ezekiel hasn't proven himself. He's a newb. I can't trust that he won't die. And I can't be sure I'll always be there to save his ass.

The thought needles at me, piercing deeper and deeper until that's all there is. Nope I absolutely cannot let myself care about this one stupid, idiot of a man. Not gonna happen. I won't let it.

With firm conviction in mind and fading in heart I scoot the parasite towards the couch and resume watch.

Steeped in darkness
I found solace from
the world. The chaos
stilled when nights
black cloak hung
around me.

Chapter 13

By the time morning comes I'm stiff. Lead weighs down my limbs and iron holds my neck straight. I wouldn't be at all surprised if I'm nailed to the chair for all the movement I'm capable of.

The others remain fast asleep. I don't disturb them. I crave silence and the outside. As much as I hate waking up, it's that moment right at dawn when the sun rises and brings with it a beautiful array of warm colors that I love most. The air still has a chill to it from the night before. Grass is slick and wet from dew. And in spite of the permanent layer of dust that coats the sky, if I close my eyes and focus on the warmth of the sun I can pretend like today is just any other day of the Before. A day where I'd wake up, get ready, and go to school to devour knowledge. A day where Mom and Dad and Annabelle would say prayers with me at the table before we ate whatever delicious concoction Mom thought up.

Moments like these last for so very little amount of time that I've learned to savor them for what they are; precious.

Enjoying this beautiful reprieve for as long as I can with a clear conscience, I take deep breathes. Inhale. One. Two. Three. Exhale. And repeat. After ten I must leave. I don't want to, but we have ground to cover before dark falls. Having others to watch out for is taxing. If it were me, alone on my bike, I'd cover the five day trip in two. But it's not.

Today I know I must talk to them. I can only be sullen for so long. As the pink fades to what I assume is a beautiful blue, I head back into my destiny. Judging by the bickering that's already ensuing I must have done something terrible in my past life.

Cara is the loudest among the bunch. "I called that!!!"

Liath is second. "I touched it first." He's not yelling like her but his voice is most certainly raised. Probably so he can be heard over all the chaos.

Mackenzie's in the mix somewhere. "Guys, please stop."

Rudy laughs in the background. "They won't listen. Especially Cara. She's a dog with a bone."

And then there's Dylan rolling his eyes and swooping in, taking whatever the idiots are foolishly fighting over.

From the couch Annabelle witnesses the act and suppresses a giggle.

To think this insanity is what I call family. Even Ezekiel's joined the bunch, "ladies and germs the candy bar's gone."

At the same time, Cara and Liath flip around to stare at the now empty counter, "What?!"

Disbelief fades into anger.

"You!" Cara accuses.

Liath counters, "You!"

Licking his chocolate covered fingers Dylan smugly announces, "Me."

The red head and the brunette exchange a look. Through their eyes they speak and seem to come to an agreement. At once they pounce on the traitor bringing him to the ground. There they became a mess of tangled limbs and curse words. I smile. Ezekiel looks stunned, his eyes flitting from one person to the next, finding no one who shares in this particular emotion. When those brilliant orbs find me I'm sucked in.

"Is this normal?" he asks.

Still sucked in I nod and reply, "As it gets." Following it up with a shrug that seemed to say "what can you do?".

Stepping over the writhing forms I make my way to the cabinet I'd scavenged the night before. The two boxes of oatmeal remain. A total of twenty four packets between them makes three breakfasts for the eight of us. Growing up I never knew math would come in handy, but in this world where every portion matters, it does. Without care I toss the boxes on the counter, bring my thumb and forefinger to my mouth and blow. A shrill whistles fills the room and the three on the floor abruptly stop. They're well trained.

"Okay, oatmeal for breakfast. One packet each--" grumblings begin, "Guys we don't have a nearly unlimited supply anymore. If your stomachs growl they growl. You'll survive."

Assent is reached and I continue. "Eat up and gather your stuff. We meet out front in thirty."

I pull Ezekiel aside to tell him what the others already know. "One packet doesn't seem like a lot but add more water and the oats will expand."

"How'd you figure that nifty trick out?"

"I'm smart." I don't want to tell him that there were times when I'd get one meal a day. That in order to not starve I had to make it expand. Foster homes could be rough.

He takes the answer without pause and moves on. Me, well I search through the cabinets for the big pot Mackenzie used the other day. Of course she would wash, dry and put it back where she found it like someone would come back here and notice we even used it. What I find crazy keeps her sane. No judgment here. We all have our things. Hers is bubbles. Mine is blood.

Pot in hand, I fill it with water and set it on the stove to boil. The next set of objects I successfully search for is bowls. They join the oatmeal on the counter.

Slowly, at first, the hot water rises and the colder water sinks. Again and again it happens until hot water is fighting equally hot water for the top spot. Then all at once small bubbles appear and soon after big ones. The bigger they get the quicker they rotate. Top bottom. Top bottom. Slow and then all at once. Just like life. You grow up slowly, shielded from the world around you and then all at once the shield falls and every sin, deed and evil thought comes at you like a flood. I shiver in spite of myself. To hide the unwanted action I mask it in the movements of opening packets of maple oatmeal and dumping it into greenish blue ceramic bowls. Whether or not I'm successful is unknown but I assume so because no one says a word.

After every bowl has been licked cleaned and seconds repeatedly begged for and said no to, we head back out into the uncertain. Nothing of note happens on the trip. Hellions are scarce; food even scarcer. Provisions seem like the best idea we've ever had. Ram shackle houses line the streets. Dusty beat up cars line the houses. Some invade the open road. Lunch comes and goes. The further we get from home the less the wind ripping through my tangled curls feels like freedom. The lines that only yesterday blurred past me in a celebration dance now look like a call to war.

Of course when demons hide it's when I want to slaughter. What I would give for a blood bath right now. To feel my blade slice though thin skin, tough muscle, and steel bone seems like a faraway dream. Warm blood dripping over my hands taunts me. The need to kill what drove me away thrums though me. The animal inside is snarling and clawing at my insides. Suppressing it is a task that calls for all my attention.

When the sun starts creeping down the sky it's about time to turn in, my hunger un-sated. Ezekiel pulls up next to me looking at ease atop Annabelle's motorcycle, a light that shines in the impending dark.

"No where's safe enough to stop."

"I know, but it's getting dark."

"Half the doors are unhinged, the other half has no windows." He's right. House after house is depleted and broken down. Shattered glass from hundreds of windows sprinkle the sidewalks, making it a minefield. Multicolored doors lay on lawns and porches, wood pieces join the broken glass. There'd be too much to barricade. We'd be safer outside. Who knows what humans lurked on the inside. In a lot cases they're worse than demons. If and when we can avoid them we do. None of us want to start or bring up our human body count.

"We keep going. Tell the others."

He nods and rides back the way he came.

Driving at dark is dangerous. Hellions aren't the only problem. The weak light that filtered in before is weaker, almost nonexistent. We can't make out potholes, cars, broken down streetlights. It's a minefield. And that's where I come in. It's my job to mark the safest way. On the motorcycle I'm less likely to hit something. Less likely still means likely so I'm cautious. The flash light I use is helpful to this particular quest, but causes problems with others: it's a spotlight. I'm the only thing light up in miles. Demon bait.

After a few miles a signal to the others by lighting up the path with my flashlight. If they zigzag they'll make it...barely. It's a tight fit and the truck will struggle, especially with its double set of back tires.

It's slow goings but eventually they pass the tipped over street light without riding over the broken glass that fans around it and the corpses falling out of a rusty old Prius. Electric cars are useless when there's no electricity to be had. The tricky part is the bottle neck formed by more abandoned and totaled cars. The path made by another vehicle smashing through them is barely visible and riddled with more broken glass. The trick is getting away with four inflated tires. Once through this minefield we are able to travel more smoothly for what seems to be fifteen minutes until we come to promising looking dwellings.

Here there's less vandalism and discarded odds and ends to worry about. Doors appear erect and lockable. Looks like the bottle neck effect came in handy. Few people made it through without dying.

Downside: the dwellings are apartment buildings. We don't have the time to search every single complex. We'll have to just find a fairly safe one, check the ones around us, hope for the best and expect the worst. Great. The day was calm but I doubt any of us will sleep tonight. Using a pre-agreed upon signal I tell the others to park and follow me.

We make our way through the front door, weapons out and grim looks on our faces; except me. I look battle crazed with two large hunting knifes twirling around in my hands. I'm first in and while the others are cautious, I stalk through the door not careful to keep my footsteps quiet. Instead I carelessly but deliberately crush the broken bits under the weight of my favorite boots. I'm the predator here and I want all to know it.

Ezekiel, to my right, is watching my every move an odd expression on his face. It isn't exactly horror but something along those lines. Liath, on my left, just rolls his eyes and takes Dylan with him to the first apartment they see.

Ideally we'd like to be on the first floor and that's our goal. The first apartments in sight will be searched. If decent we'll bunk here for the night. A couple signals and Rudy's off with Ezekiel

They head to the apartment on the right. Cara, who waits patiently behind me, follows me to the apartment directly in front of us. The doors slightly ajar, not a good sign. Other than Annabelle, Cara and I work best together in situations like these. Neither of us fear. Whatever's behind that door we will both face it with equal fever. Back to back we will slice down anything with claws. She's the only one who enjoys the hunt as much as I do.

Together we push through the door, me in the lead. Scanning the area quickly I spot two Scavengers over what was once a human in the living room and another in the kitchen. And while they dismiss us almost instantly we still have to kill them. Their noise will attract attention.

Graceful as a feline, I leap over the broken coffee table, wield my blades like an expert and slice them to pieces. The first dies of a cut to the throat. The second I filet like a fish: stomach to chest. Cara dispenses the last one and we are done.

Twisted grins on our blood spattered faces, we head to the next room.

After two empty rooms I begin to feel hopeless. I'd thought we'd be able to burn off more steam then a couple Scavengers. They aren't even a challenge. By the fourth room I've lost the pep to my step and the cheery smile on my face. Surprisingly, Cara's more optimistic.

"Cheer up! This is going to be a good one."

Not agreeing I let her go first. It's the worst mistake of the day. Six Corpse Eaters hunch over the new remains of a Scavenger. They're different in that Corpse Eaters are vultures and Scavengers are decomposers. Their faces are gnarly and teeth form in more places than their one apparent mouth. They are everywhere, used for scraping every bit of flesh and tendon from bone. The sea of teeth – sharper than any nail -- is the challenge I'd been hoping for.

Cara grabs the leader before I can. Bitch. The second biggest one is mine. My thoughts get in the way of action and I have to duck an unexpected cheap shot or risk getting beheaded. The air that slides by my face and lifts my hair from the missed blow sends my adrenaline through the roof. It's on.

Using the duck I get into the creatures personal space and land a slice on his abdomen. Not liking that I drew first blood, the stupid thing lunges straight at me. His body weight...if it's a he...I'm pretty sure, gives me the strength I need, without wasting any of my own precious energy, to slide the knife in and up. Once it reaches where his heart presumably is, I twist. A guttural noise passes between his muted green lips and that's it. Another goner.

Both Cara and I are down one with two more to go. To my surprise the next two are more worthy opponents than the first. They aren't as big, not even close, but they're smarter. Together they attempt to corner me. One comes from the left: employing a slow, easy gait in attempts to hide its excitement. It's over eagerness spells death. Her (I've decided it's a she) life meets its end by Cara's stealthy blade. The next is all mine. There's nothing unsuspecting about it.

The attempt fails but at least they tried. Props for that.

We've all finished our rooms and regroup in one of the few that are corpse free and demonless. Mackenzie brings Belle in and all weary faces turn to me. Those of us, save Cara and myself, who were on Death Duty look exhausted. They --Ezekiel, Rudy, Liath, and Dylan-- will have first crack at shut eye. Mackenzie and Belle will follow. Cara and I, newly rejuvenated by fresh blood, will take first watch.

"You four grab a place and nap. No showers," I say. Places like this are too dangerous for the *pitter patter* of water from a shower head. And the *splash* as it falls from damp hair to porcelain is a calling card.

"No lights either." Too many creepy crawlers. In the fifteen or so rooms we scanned at least fifty demons were discovered and slaughtered. Most were lower level, but still. Apartments, with so many possible nesting options, are the worst camp grounds. We'd be better off in the woods with sleeping bags.

The boys shuffle off, fatigue lining every inch of them. They can hardly put one foot in front of the other. Too bad sleep is unlikely. I want them to try, but chances of success are slim.

"Do you think they'll actually sleep?" Cara, surprisingly, is on the same page as me.

"I hope so."

"I wouldn't be able to. Not with where we are."

She twitches in spite of herself. She's afraid. We all are. Our lives wouldn't be described as easy, let alone safe, but what we had at least permitted sleep. This was an insomniac's playground.

I say, "Let's hope they can."

If survival were an option
she'd just as soon tear out
her own heart and destroy it
than live with its misguided
attempts to bring her happiness.

Chapter 14

An hour and a half passes with no sound but even breathing and sleepless rustling. The guys had stilled for maybe all of twenty minutes or so before jolting awake, checking their surrounding and laying back down to toss and turn some more. They're devoted fellas. Roughing through it and accepting any scrap of sleep the Sand Man allows. I'm envious.

I can feel exhaustion's noose tightening around my throat and crushing my trachea, but I'm helpless. Sleep wouldn't come even if I was able to patiently wait for it. I can see Cara's in the same boat as me, but fear of attracting the unwanted to our temporary safe haven keeps me from speaking.

Bored, I sit quietly and watch the others. Liath's chest is rising and falling, his lungs expanding and contracting in the slow pattern that declares sleep. Good for him.

Rudy lies on his stomach and then flips to his back, an exasperated sigh slipping out. Poor boy. Having given up, Dylan twiddles his thumbs -- one rolling over the other continuously-- and stares blankly at the yellowing popcorn ceiling.

Ezekiel's with Dylan: done trying. He stares off into space, a glossy sheen over his eyes as he relives another time. Perhaps he is back in wartime watching his comrades die beside him or back waking up to find his "brother" gone. I spend a quarter of an hour creating scenarios in my head:

Ezekiel packing, saying goodbye to his loved ones; Rudy included and maybe a girlfriend, who knew, and heading off to an unknown he thought better than the known. Grass is always greener.

Him finding out, all by himself, that in fact the grass is bloodier on the other side. Or him making it through a year after the horrible revelation, before being joined by Rudy. I wonder if he told him of the horrors. Did he warn him what watching a fellow soldier bleed to death could do to a man? Did he explain what it is to see someone mowed down by a semi-automatic machine gun? To be the person doing the mowing? Did he say anything at all or was he selfish?

I want to ask, but I don't. It's not my place. Not yet. I have to earn it first.

Moving on: Mackenzie and Annabelle appear to be the only ones making the best of a crappy situation. Belle sits in the cheap looking muted green couch, her leg propped up by an equally ugly beige pillow, looking more herself than the day before. Each mile away from home she looks better. I look worse. Her cheeks still puffy with baby fat gain the color of dawn while mine become shallow. As her eyes gain the twinkle of the stars brave enough to shine through the smoke, mine become shaded and dark. Belle gains strength, I lose mine. Loss of fear and worry? It flies off her shoulders and lands its punishing weight on mine. Better her than me. Always.

Mackenzie sits next to her, a book stabilizing a piece of paper in their hands. Based on the look of concentration on her; squinting eyes and sucked in bottom lip, they're playing a game and she's losing.

Like a creep I watch them for a bit. Silently I decide the victors of each game. If I base it on the amount of times each had their constipation concentration face in place then Belle's in the lead: 7-2. Whatever they are playing Kenzie's no good.

Cara's doing what I'm doing: people watching. She turns her attention to me and I wave. She suppresses a sincere giggle.

Looking at the clock above the doorway I find I've spent a little over an hour people watching. It's not even midnight. Another six more hours before we can leave this place.

Boredom taking hold I start acting weird. First thing on the list is looking at my nose and seeing if I'm able to drag my eyes upwards and stare at my eyebrows. No such luck. Next, air in the cheeks. Smack those suckers and repeat. When that becomes old, and it does so quickly, it's seeing if I can look at my top and bottom lip, respectively. This I can do. But being crossed eyed too long brings on a headache so I stop.

Only to find an audience of seven amused faces watching me. Flipping them the bird only brings held in laughter. Sticking my tongue out garners the same results.

"Oh shut up!" I'm the first to break the silence in nearly four hours.

The compulsive action isn't enough to break open the gates. But the locks?

They're gone. Liath, awoken hungry, fetches the backpack full of food from the front door. Deliberate quiet settles as we mechanically pass around bags of food -- jerky, freeze dried strawberries and bananas, trail mix – and chew.

Another forty five minutes pass and we are twitching. We won't survive another five minutes of silence. Five hours is out of the question. There's nothing to do but talk and we're too anxious to do that. Sleep's a faraway dream. Unattainable except in twenty or thirty minutes increments. Safety was a thing we underappreciated before. Never again.

Law-abiding, rule-following Kenzie comes to the conclusion that now is a perfectly acceptable time to trade in those goodie two shoes for bad girl boots. "So what's the first thing you guys want to experience when we get to Caelo?"

Stunned but not stupid we pull on our own bad boots and follow her willingly. "Sleep." Liath says.

"What?! Like you don't get enough now, lug head. You'd sleep through an earthquake--"

"Or better yet, an apocalypse." Dylan and Belle tease.

Liath plays along. "Oh shut up guys." But then gets suddenly serious. "You can't tell me you've had a fear free night since this all began." Earnestly he searches our expressions, hoping to find he's not alone. He isn't.

"I haven't," I admit.

"Nope," chimes in Belle.

Rudy says, "Not I."

"Me neither," Cara agrees.

"Since longer than all this," Dylan confirms.

"My whole life," Mackenzie whispers.

Unwilling to let this moment sour, I joke, "so who do you think will haunt your nightmares once we're safe, Cara or the demons?"

Mock contemplation settles across his face, his pointer finger goes up to tap his chin and his eyes roll up and to the left. Finally, "Cara."

Cara, for the first time, doesn't throw a rude comment his way. She laughs instead, surprising us all nearly as much as Mackenzie did.

Directing the flow of conversation Rudy asks, in his usual brotherly teasing way, "Okay Cara, what's the first thing you'd want to do?"

A smile, all teeth, carves its way across Cara's hollow cheeks. It tells us all we need to know; wherever her dreams take her bloods involved...and not hers. "Fight club." Her jack-o-lantern smile matches her flames for eyes. I suppose it wasn't the apocalypse that made her all sharp edges and gunslinger attitude. That was just Cara.

"Creeeppy." Dylan drags out with a shudder, producing yet another round of laughs from his light hearted audience.

When our chuckles calm and giggles fade, Cara grabs hold of the proverbial microphone, "So big brother, what will you do?" And points it at Rudy.

Uncomfortable with attention Rudy writhes and squirms in his seat. "Um, well I guess I'd go back to the army and try to extend my leave further--"

"I thought you were a deserter!" I blurt out thoughtlessly. Me and my big mouth.

Un-offended, Rudy answers the unasked question, "God no. I got extended leave due to family matters. It also helped them out because they wanted eyes on the inside and I was the only volunteer."

"Until me."

"Yeah, you idiot. You just had to follow me," Rudy chastises Ezekiel.

He shrugs his shoulders in response. "You're all the family I have. You left me with no other option."

Pained Rudy says, "But you're a deserter now Zeke. That means prison."

Zeke (apparently) laughs. He actually laughs. Out loud. In Rudy's rueful gaze. Rudy, however, doesn't bristle. It's obvious they've known each other a long ass time because of any of us had done that? Not good.

"I'm not idiot. Not a deserter either."

"How?"

"Remember our Christmas leave?"

"Yeah?"

They continue to ping pong back and forth -- Zeke, Rudy, Zeke, Rudy-- the rest of us left confused. "Well when I found out where your sorry ass ran off to, I switched mine with Cross. He was more than happy to spend Christmas with his wife and baby."

"Oh."

"Yeah."

"We're good?" Rudy confirms.

"Yes," affirms Ezekiel.

Cara, the petulant little sister at heart -- by only eleven months as she likes to remind us -- cuts of their bro-convo, and clears the floor for Dylan. "So what about you, D? What will you do?"

"A movie sounds nice." This he directs at all of us. "With a beautiful girl by my side," he says solely to Cara.

Blood suffuses through her hollow checks. Though she's been oddly friendly and full of humor, no one says a word. You poke the bear enough and it won't be Pooh you'll be getting.

Sensing the same thing as me, Kenzie tells us all what she plans on doing. Hers is the most predictable. "If Caelo is really a safe haven than the waters must be safe too, right?" None of us dare to be the one to burst her bubble so we silently nod as she continues. "So that means no murderous Sirens eager to drag me into oblivion," unconsciously Mackenzie's green streaked hazel eyes find me, her mind picturing the gruesome scars that mare my legs. Others would think they stole beauty from me, but I and the rest of the girls know they gave me strength.

"If that's true," she continues after a brief apologetic pause towards me and my memories, "then I'd grab the first board I could find, slap on some wax, throw on a bathing suit, and surf. What'd I'd give to feel the waves rolling beneath me and the salty air stinging my face? I'd die for chapped lips."

"I prefer your lips smooth," says Rudy as he swoops in for a kiss. And not a quick one. Tongue and all. I'm jealous of them and their openness.

Mackenzie's giggles pierce the air and I avert my eyes. Someday. It's what I keep telling myself. Once her giggles turn into breathy sighs all eyes turn to me.

Genuinely curious, for we have never discussed an end to our Hell, Annabelle asks, "Leila?" The rest of the question is implied.

I'd sincerely hoped they'd forget about me. Move on to Annabelle and forget I haven't answered. But I'll tell the truth even if I don't want to. I'm a terrible liar. All previous attempts ended in gross disappointments. Not to mention, deceit makes my stomach churn.

"Don't judge," I say.

"No promises." Cara answers at the same time Dylan states, "I always do." The sarcastic bastards are perfect for each other.

"And this is why I don't like telling you baboons anything."

Bell like laughter falls from Annabella's pale pink lips. "Baboons?"

"Idiots?" I amend.

"Imbeciles." Rudy adds.

"El stupido," says Mackenzie proudly.

I list, "Jerks. Bitches. Asshats."

Cara says, "Dumbasses."

"Butts." Coming from the creative Liath.

"Brainless," I throw out.

"Butts for brains," Liath says between chuckles.

Breathless and achy, I stop them before I start to cry. "Okay, okay, yes all those things."

"Hey!" Ezekiel interrupts, "What about me?"

Flirtatious hurt pulls at his moist lower lip. Mock offense widens his eyes, exposing more of the green that captivates me. Whether it's these distractions or another unaccounted for issue that causes me to worry my cheek with my sharp canines, I don't know, but I do know they need to stop.

Attempting to make him suck his lip back up and let his eyelids drop I say, with unintended coquettishness, "While I'm sure you're much like the others, for now you're pardoned pending an investigation."

His lips divide as my sentence ends; however, they close again and silence descends. That is until Annabelle, graciously, reminds me of the question at hand. Sealing up the *"I hate you"* response I'm eager to give, I answer, reluctantly, "I want to go back to school."

Liath throws back his head, red hair following suit and chuckles like I've said something funny. I'd give him a reason to laugh. "You'll be going to school too Chuckles." That killed his mirth.

"Ooh she told you." Annabelle, like Liath, needs to learn to zip her lip.

"Don't worry, sweets, you'll be joining him."

She cries out, "What? Why?!"

"How old are you?" A question as an answer.

Like a brat she says, "You know how old I am."

"Indulge me."

"Fifteen."

"So that makes you a sophomore this year, right?" I ask the unwilling crowd. They hate our verbal clashes almost as much as I do.

To my dismay it's Belle's protector who speaks up. "Yes, and I'll be a junior."

Not allowing the unexpected turn of events throw me off, I forge ahead. "Yes, thank you! Belle, you honestly believe I gave you all those lessons so you could skip school?"

"No," she answers sullenly.

"Exactly. So school."

"Okay," the youngest answer in accord.

Perceiving the end of the sister war, Ezekiel asks, "What do you want to be?"

It's the perfect question and one I've only answered for myself. A weight lifts off my shoulder, lightening my immense burden, when I answer, "An author or a teacher of sorts."

Intrigued and a bit stung that I've never confided in her, Belle asks, "In what subject?" The sparkle in her eyes, while beautiful and a sign of health earlier, stabs at me.

I attempt a lie to assuage the guilt, "I never said anything before because I'm undecided."

Like a lycanthrope she sniffs out the lie and howls on. "But if you had to choose."

Disinclined to unsheathe my proverbial swords I settle for an answer. "English or mythology."

"Cool," inserts Rudy. "Which kind?"

"Not sure. Anything end of the world-y."

Cara, a look of attitude back on her sharp features, asks, "Seriously?"

Before I can answer, with my own air of haughtiness, a group of demons attracted by our failed attempt at stealth burst through the kitchen window. We should've gone up a floor.

The moon: a constant

reminder that

darkness is never

all encompassing.

Chapter 15

Lured into a false sense of security the attack takes us by surprise and we scramble for the weapons on our person. Rebounding with haste I'm up first. *Zing*. Air makes way for death as a steel topped bolt embeds itself in a Nightmares' pitch black eye. Heat flies by my face, infusing my check with color before finding its way into the epicenter of a Soul Eater's forehead. I reach up to check my cheek. My fingers come back clean, the bullet hadn't grazed me.

Its barracuda-like jaw yawns open in surprise, the glint of faded light in thousands of teeth its final farewell. Lower level hellions -- Scavengers, Corpse Eaters, Body Stealers, and the nameless -- saddle their way over the window sill and into a war zone. Cara zooms by, blades twirling in her hands. Dylan follows suit, axe an extended part of his body hacking through demons.

Liath, my savior, backs Annabelle into a corner and starts shooting at anything that gets close. Belle looks sore at being defended, but she's alive to do so. Mackenzie defends Rudy's flank with her choice of weapon; an AR-15. And while it sucks at close combat like this, she's found a way around that tiny insignificant fact: bash them over the head with the butt, repeatedly if necessary. Rudy's got Kenzie's six covered with his Glock. A heap of demons, bullets in their brains, act as an impromptu barrier in front of him.

That leaves myself and Ezekiel who looks to me for instruction. I toss one of my many guns to him and keep the crossbow. Together we work as a unit, more deadly than the other pairs. Even as Body Stealers send in their undead minions we don't lose ground. In fact we gain some.

Every inch brings us closer to our destination: the window. If we make it we gain the upper hand. Mowed down by the sheer unexpected force of eight humans, some demons tuck tail (literally) and run. Others, more brave or stupid, stay and fight.

With less claws at my throat I'm able to observe. The demons, all of different breed and race, work together towards one objective: me. While the others get some action, most of them turn their beady eyes my way. They don't appear threatening either. They fall as their brothers fell, too easily.

An idea forms and I seize it before is dissipates. "Guys, go!"

They protest, as I knew they would. Unable to confess the true seed of my plan I tell them another, very probable reason. "We're trapped unless one of us plays jester. They're single minded. If I stay, you guys can make it out of here." My statement is punctuated by a *zing* through the air and a gush of deep purple blood from an unsuspecting demons neck. "I can hold them long enough to free you."

"What about you?!" Annabelle cries.

"C'mon Belle, you know me." The *I'll survive* is left unspoken.

"I'll stay," offers Ezekiel.

That won't work. "No. Rudy and you will carry Belle." Before she can object I add, "For this to work I need to know you're safe."

Wheat tresses bounce as she nods. "Cara you're point. Dylan you're rear. Liath and Kenzie defend three and nine."

Looks of hesitation start to form so I give them a push, "Rudy, your extra gun please?" He hands it over, desperation spurring him forward and casting his bear-like eyes in a dark glare.

He pulls out extra clips and hands them to me too. "You know how to work it?" He's stalling.

Accommodating him, I nod. "Now go. Before it's too late. Radio when you're safe." Without last looks they're gone. This isn't goodbye.

I turn to the horde in front of me and move on auto-pilot. Every bolt I have left on my person *zings* through the air to find its way into a demon. Fatal wounds only. The ground beneath them riddled with corpses and slick with multicolored blood doesn't slow them down. They keep coming. All eyes on me. Some even hiss, growl, bellow, snarl or moan my name. It's a chorus of mal-purpose.

Quiver empty and unable to switch to my gun just yet, I grab a blade from each of my sleeves. Both find and stop their targets before they can finish shimming over the window sill.

At last a break in the mob appears and I'm able to load a clip in the Glock, turn off the safety and fire until I hear a *click*.

Somewhere in the background an engine roars to life. And another. And one more. They made it, but they aren't out of the woods just yet. Another clip slammed into the chamber successes the first.

More bodies fall. Some creatures get too close for comfort as others watch me too intently. I'm eager to know what they want from me, but not that eager.

Out of bullets and blades, I switch tactics and employ the blunt edge of Rudy's Glock. The pause in artillery spray allows three nasty suckers a chance to gain footing on the solid ground in front of me. A flurry of motion and three crushed skulls later and I bolt for the door, praying no more opponents stand in my way.

Through the threshold and I move on. I skid around the corner, paying no mind to the intersecting halls. Eyes only for the spider webbed glass double doors beyond. I'm blindsided.

Limbs flail as a solid object meets my middle. My building momentum changes course and sends me cartwheeling to the side; a flurry of arms and legs. Dazed I lay there, glass grinding against the exposed skin, a moment longer than is safe.

Clawed digits yank me to a standing position. Blood beads in the crescent wounds, bubbles up and spills over. My mind follows the path of crimson as it slithers down my arms and soaks my fingertips. The slippery liquid worms its way between the Glock and the cage that is my fingers.

As my body races to catch up with my mind, I face my opponent, sizing him up. And trust me, it's a him. No question about it. His wolfish face – grotesquely extended jaw, sunken in cheeks, large eyes and pointed ears – tells all I need to know. Lycanthrope. And not a stupid one. His luminous amber eyes shine with the intelligence of an Alpha.

My outsmarting him is unlikely. His animal nature added to the intelligence of a man makes him a deft adversary. Plus he has a foot on my 5'3" frame and biceps that could pulverize my skull. Brute strength won't get me far, but unfortunately at the moment that's all I got.

If I can stun him, 10 to 1 I can outrun him. What I lack in strength I make up for in speed. Though his legs are significantly longer than mine, I'm likely quicker. Better be because I'm betting my life on it.

The polymer frame of the gun sings a high pitched song in my hand. "*Use me! Use me!*" Joining the chorus, the metal parts on the inside. Their baritone voices promise pain and violence. They can and will help me escape.

Accepting their assistance, I slam the heel of my chunky boots on Wolf Man's instep. A howl escapes him, echoing through the hall and beyond. Urgency becomes everything now. The last thing I need is for his brainless buddies to show up and cause more havoc.

My adversary releases my arms to grab for his throbbing foot. Without further delay I smash the crooning gun into his thick skull. Another yowl impregnates the silent night with noise. Unwilling to be around when he comes out of his Leila induced stupor, I dart through the door.

Outside no eyes look my way. Idiocy comes in spades with most demons and they're more concerned with where I was than where I am. Thanking the cloudless sky above me and whomever it cloaks behind its shadows, I mount my bike and take off.

As it becomes apparent that the gang mowed through any and all obstacles, leaving the road navigable and without impediment, I'm grateful. Starting up my bike and taking off the way I did created quite a bit of racket as my engine worked overtime to follow the speedometer. It's plausible that the noise – cranking of gears and pushing of pistons – would attract attention from the not-so-brainless bunch in the crowd of idiots. Unable to spare time to look back, I step on it and let the night blur by at top speed.

At this speed everything looks different. The speckled yellow lines turn into one continuous arrow pointing towards safety. Solid road melts into a black tumultuous river. One wrong move and lights out. Winter bares the trees and the branches dance sinuously, beckoning the wanderer into their maze of death. Once in there is no return from the barren land free of animals and sustenance. Moonlight beams down on the scene, washing out the shadowed green of the pines as they flow into a tapestry of color; light greens and forest, shadowed and faded.

Before long static joins the cacophony of sound – howling wind, snapping twigs, and shattering frost. Dylan's voice breaks the static. "Leila?"

"Here."

"Safe?"

"Yes." Radio time is information only time. No telling when the static will reign.

"Follow the destruction to a clearing on the side of the road. Someone will be waiting for you."

"Copy."

Returning my hand back to the handle bars I allow myself a cursory glance behind me. Nothing save for branches stir. I'm truly alone with my thoughts. Not a creature stirring and all that bullshit. Oh the holiday spirit.

I hate, to a degree I didn't know was possible, when my mind wanders. That place, my mind, is a twisted labyrinth full of dark corners and vortexes that turn me inside out and with no end in sight. Behind every bend lurks a fear. Through every door a doubt. The sky rains hate and the ground trembles with jealousy. In my own little inferno I recede. All noise falls away. Everything but my bike and destination fades into obscurity as hell's fingers grip tight.

In a matter of days everything I knew to be true began to fracture and crumble. Worse than that, it would appear the truth hid in the people I never wanted to meet. The truth of who I was, and I can admit at least subconsciously, to a greater degree what.

I'd thought Annabelle a fool when she went off spouting nonsense about hellions after me. Chalked it up to a moment of irrational fear. The fight tonight proved me wrong and her right. All the others faced vicious opponents out for blood, but not me. My attackers were less deadly and more fascinated. They meticulously watched my every move. Every pivot, throw of blade or pull of trigger. All multicolored eyes were riveted on me. As if I were a ballerina and they the captive audience gasping at every leap and twirl. Or an experiment with them playing scientists. A giggle claws up my throat at the ridiculous thought of demons in glasses and white coats. With sheer will as my only ally I shove it back into the depths of me.

Truly, watching as my family met unrelenting after unrelenting wave of spawns was maddening. Being witness and witness only to the harsh way those creatures attacked drove my insides out. Especially when it became clear that compared to their attackers mine treated me like a porcelain doll. That is until I found an advantage to their delicacy.

It was only a guess, a suspicion that seeded in my gut and blossomed to a flower in my mind. I wanted to believe the seed planted itself tonight and grew because of overwhelming evidence, but it did not. The little bugger set up residence yesterday when I saw my reflection in the mirror. The apparition staring back at me belonged with the demons outside. Crimson spider webs etched their way across the eyes surface, glaring against the white background. Opaque flesh becomes the backdrop to still lips. Soaked ebony tendrils paint along the canvas that is shoulders. Black and white. More haunting than striking.

While cold houses itself in the very bones that keep her form she is unaffected. Not a shutter ripples through her body. But if you follow the veins until they reach the hands and fingers, there a never ending shake resides. Chattering teeth refuse to echo throughout the chilly bathroom. She's still. Horrifyingly so. It's like she's not surprised. She's been aware of the monsters hiding just below the entire time.

I 'spose I already knew the truth as well, but I buried it so far inside me I forgot. It took a memory from the past – my sixteenth birthday – to awaken the secret inside me. The hoodies and glasses not only hid me from the world but also my true nature from myself.

Why else would the hellions be interested in me? And for a reason that didn't involve picking my remains from their teeth. I must be of their ilk. The thought sends my meager dinner churning; the mere idea blasphemy.

Any further thoughts come to a halt at the flicker of a flashlight beam about ten yards ahead of me and to my left. I signal back: turning off my headlight and on again. Once. Twice. Three times.

Pulling up to the clearing in the copse of trees I shut off the engine and deploy the kickstand. What greets me is not what I expect – Rudy lecturing me about putting myself in needless danger and how we are a team and should work together and everything else he's always yammering on about – and steel myself for. It's far from it. Figures rush me in the hazy light. If not for knowing it's my friends, I'd instantly transition into the defensive.

Arms flail trying to reach me. Annabelle the first, undeterred by her injury. Her slight frame hides the muscle she reveals in her bone crushing hug. Lilacs and violets, their innocent scent, fruity and fresh flows over me. It's the scent I've always associated with Belle. Not a perfume or a lotion; just her. I inhale deeply, holding the aroma inside me as the next person moves in.

The shocking red hair and towering frame marks the person as Liath. He bundles me in his arms and whispers in my ear, "Belle was worried sick."

Tears prick my eyes. She may still be mad but she cares. The others swarm in one by one, even Cara and Ezekiel to my surprise. I know when the latter wraps his arms around me. It's like being hit by a lightning bolt, but instead of being charred the electricity runs through me. The shock jerks me to life. Atom by atom feeling returns. I gasp in spite of myself. I haven't felt this alive, in touch with someone in years.

But it's like my body already knows him. My curves fit in to all his angles, my head falls right at his heart, the *thump-dum thump-dum thump-dum* echoing my own. He pulls back, a smirk on his face. It's clear the sensation wasn't felt by me alone. Finally.

While I could look into those eyes forever, following the swirls of green down a path to happiness, now is not the time. So I ask, "What's the plan?"

See me. Please. Allow me to kneel

before you, claw open my rib cage, and

expose the horrors that live inside. A

soul so entwined with shadows, extraction

is impossible.

I beg you, see me. Let me plunge my hand

into the gaping hole, remove my heart, and

bare it to you. Show you all the hideous flaws

and disfigurements that mar it.

See me. Know me. Understand me. I beseech

you. Shed light on the dark that inhabits me.

Spread balm on the injuries. Heal all my

broken.

Chapter 16

Someone hands me a piece of jerky to gnaw on as Rudy lays out the plan for tonight. "No guards," far enough away from the demons to not worry about that, "but no fires either," but close enough to fear attracting the hellion horde with the bright palette associated with warmth. Tonight was not going to be fun.

"We leave at first light," Rudy states.

"Seriously, bro?" Cara complains like usual. Nice to see things haven't changed along with our environment.

"Yes."

For once Liath is on Cara's side, "but we gained so much ground tonight. Can't you give us a little time in the morning?"

"We don't want to lose that ground," Rudy says. It's final.

I groan along with everyone else. My body is aching in places I didn't know existed. The threat of death can take a lot out of a person.

The thought morphing into one of sleep I get comfortable on the hard packed earth. Too tired to unroll a sleeping bag or pay attention to the rock beneath me. Hands cradling head, left ankle crossed over right, I fade from the world.

⚥　⚥　⚥　⚥　⚥

"Not a monster. Not a monster."

Tremors rock the ground, tossing my body forward – lips kissing the dirt – and back again. The rolling of the ground yanks me from my nightmare and throws me back into reality.

Glancing up I find the viridescent eyes of the earthquake boring into the blue of my own. Ezekiel. Irritated, I rub sleep from my eyes only to find, much to my embarrassment, paths of dried tears chapping my smooth flesh.

Attempting to hide the signs of weakness staining my face, I sidle into my armor of sarcasm and bitchy comments. Cattiness don't fail me now. "The moons up, why am I?"

Pointedly twin glacial flames flicker to the robust sphere aglow in the twilight.

Pale blue; the sign of hidden truths at the least and out right deceit at the most.

Ezekiel refuses to bow to my barriers and rips the shield of sarcasm from my dainty hands and probes my aura of fear. "Who's not the monster? You?" He's too damn perceptive for my own good.

The pale blue is here to stay. "I don't know what you are talking about." As the words slip between my lips my eyes turn to icicles, nearly see through. The daggers of ice find their target and hone in. He takes in the look with twin flames of his own – as chartreuse as mine are cerulean – and still opens his moist lips.

"Liar."

The word stings though he speaks the truth. It's one I've been called all my life: when I told the truth. Even after a year away from civilization I can't shake the slime of disgust that settles over every inch of me at the sound of that one word.

Unwilling to fulfill its definition, I backtrack. "Okay I do know what you're talking about. I just want to keep my secrets my secrets."

Air lays sentient in my lungs. Waiting. Will he let it slide? Or push?

The moments after I wake from the living hell that is sleep are the worst. Most mornings I lay in bed reminding myself it's only a nightmare. The tortures dispensed aren't truly by my hands. I wouldn't, couldn't hurt those I love like that. Even the ones I detest would meet a better fate.

I'm no sadist. Bloodthirsty? Yes. But meticulous in pain? No. Pulling finger nails from skin isn't up my alley. Nor is delicately crushing every bone in a hand. It's gruesome, despicable work. Not me.

To my relief he lets it be. For now. Imploringly his eyes seek mine, compassion swirling in the kaleidoscope of greens. My own version of eye catcher churns as well: dark and deep like the ocean during a storm.

"I'm here to talk. When and if you're ever ready." Something he sees must trigger his protective nature. And while I like to think I'm in no need of protection I'm thankful for his offer. "Now back to bed. I'll keep the nightmares at bay." If only he knew.

Reluctantly, I lay back on the dirt and grass below me. The pebble from earlier remains wedged beneath me. Again I'm too preoccupied to give it much notice. A bug of sorts crawls across the flesh not covered by my shirt. Its tiny legs feather light. The creature stops those six legs; if I counted correctly, still as the wind around us. Not a movement before another substance – gossamer like – tickles me and then in a poof, gone.

Try as I might, sleep won't come. Closing my eyes and allowing the sounds of the woods to soothe me is fruitless. Sleep just won't come. Abandoned by the Sand Man I'm left to my memories.

Eyes find the sky but see nothing. The beauty of the moon penetrates not. The cloak of blackness roams not. I'm elsewhere: where Belle sits in a chair – restrained and gagged – sweat drenches her wheat hair and color drains from her face.

Those cornflower blue eyes beg for release, for death. But I'm the punisher and mercy isn't in my nature. If not for the filthy balled up soak stuffed between her chapped and cracking lips, soul wrenching screams would echo throughout this damp dungeon.

Water trickles down the jutted stone walls of the cavernous space, instigating the moss below to grow and flourish as I bring a hammer down on Annabelle's knee; a ruthless light in my eyes. At her muffled scream everything changes. In an instant it's no longer my sister with rope burns on her wrist and ankles but Rudy.

Unlike Belle who whimpered away from me and my cruelty Rudy is all malice. He'll kill me if he breaks free of the bonds that dig into his pink flesh; shredding skin and drawing blood every time he breathes. This time I know I'll have to be more ruthless. He'll be a hard cookie to break. Broken knee caps won't do him in.

Languidly, I trace my fingers over the beloved tools of the trade. In reality they're tools you'd find in any working man's tool box – wrenches and drills, screw drivers and box cutters and pliers – like my Dad's. The pliers call out to me; a hum of finger nails sliding out of skin and screams piercing the night.

For fun I remove his gag. Hate makes him spit at me. Not missing a beat I back hand him across the face. Crimson spittle spews from his split lip. I got him good, but not good enough.

"You'll pay for that," I snarl as I grab for the drill.

Snap. Snap. Snap.

The brown of Rudy's eyes bore into mine and I flinch before I can stop myself. If he notices he doesn't say.

"Good morning, sunshine, the earth says hello."

"And Leila says bite me."

A good hearted chuckle escapes him and I barely override the need to recoil. I am a monster. The benevolent look in his eyes flickers to hate as my twisted imagination fuses with reality.

"Is she up?" Belle calls from her spot near the SUV. Her bell-like voice – the affectionate nickname isn't solely derived from her name but also from the lovely timbre of her voice – breaks through my haze and brings me to the world where demons are on our tails; with a special interest in yours truly, where we are trekking through hell to reach the devil; otherwise known as the biologicals, and where we vent by slaughtering hellions. And to think that's what is real. My torturing Rudy seems more plausible.

Accepting his outstretched hand I pull myself off the uncomfortable ground. Kinks groan everywhere as I turn this way and that, loosening up. My muscles scream in protest at the thought of another full day of riding. Fire claimed my thighs during the night and ice had frozen my back stiff.

Noticing my aches Liath offers to take the bike. "You want the SUV?"

He'd rather not switch. That much is obvious. Annabelle's on the mend in the hulking gas guzzler. The protector in him wants to snuggle her close and not let her go. Especially while out here in the danger zone.

"Nah I'm good."

"You sure?" His protector instinct appears to extend to me.

I nod. And with that he hops up into the vehicle, a smile on his face. Puppy love. For their sake I hope it lasts.

"Hungry?" asks Mackenzie.

"Starved." She hands me a can of beans. The warmth seeps through my palms and expels the chill of the night. And while it's not the most appealing meal in the world I scarf it down. Food is food. Even if it sticks to the roof of the mouth and clogs the throat.

When the bottom of the aluminum can is in my vision, I ask to no one in particular, "When do we head out?"

"In five," Cara answers before a groan and a face behind her brother's back.

"Dirty looks don't make friends," Rudy calls without turning around.

An incredulous look plasters its way across Cara's features. I just shrug. Rudy's one crazy dude. I definitely want him on my side of the line.

Finished with the sludge we call breakfast, I mount my bike without instruction. Getting closer to the rural that separates suburban areas means more frequent stops and use of emergency supplies. Which also means, for me, socialization. There's just too much churning in my mind, volatile stuff and twisted thoughts, to sit through meals with the rest.

Somehow I'll have to make it work. But that's awhile away. Why dread the future when you can remember the past?

With every blow I hardened.

Concrete pouring into my veins

until my body became statuesque.

Only my heart remained stubborn.

Fighting the sluggish liquid with

every beat, daring to be heard

despite my mind's resistance.

Chapter 17

It's the end of August. Of summer. The last weekend and for many the last hoorah before school starts; on a Wednesday no less. But not for me. A nice book and a bubble bath sounds like the perfect send off.

Junior year. Parties and prom. Dating and driving. Every teenagers dream. Mine as well not six months ago. But so much has changed. The only staples that haven't changed or been removed are Elvira and Pinky. So when they beg me, legit beg; on their knees, one hand cupped over the other shaking, puppy dog faces in place, and a chorus of pleases to go to the beach with them it's hard to say no.

All summer I've managed to evade that catastrophe. So much skin showing to way too many people. Who knows what would happen? I attract crazies as it is with sweat pants and t-shirts two sizes too big. Those clothes won't fly where sun and sand dominate. Not only would I stick out more but I'd die of heat stroke.

Reading the big fat NO written across my face the girls' throw their stupid logic at me. "Sunglasses are beach wear."

Ahh, the precious sunglasses. Smart move on their part. Genius actually. Covering my eyes was everything to me. Few people – my family and the girls -- remained unaffected and so were allowed access. Unless an asshole teacher made me take them off I had protection everywhere. Summer, winter, fall, spring. It didn't matter.

Gaining the one up they press forward, "And you could wear a hoodie."

"And how would I work that?" I ask.

Pinky scolds dramatically, "Have you truly already forgotten all about fashion?"

"Oh the horror!" Elvira faux sobs.

"Uh no." Yes. It's now the furthest thing from my mind. What does fashion matter when you can't bear to be looked at. When it's dangerous.

As I cross the room to my closet Pinky questions, "Do you still have that woven sweater you got at the mall last year?"

"The colorful one?" I ask.

"The oversized one," adds Elvira.

They were like a dog with a bone. It was clear my mind was made up for me. I would be going to the beach.

"I'm driving," I say. Forever defiant. Even pointlessly.

Dressed to the nines we haul our load across the beach. Flip flops scattering sand behind us as we trudge through the difficult terrain. As to be expected the beach is packed. So many people I can barely breathe. This was such a stupid idea. Idiotic really.

A mob forms in my mind and attacks. I'm buried in sand. Feet all around me. My throat clogs until we walk past the first row of people. Not a person looks my way. I'm invisible.

Giddy, I laugh.

The day was the picture of perfection. High above the sun beams down on us, a caressing heat. Below us sand fills the crevices between our toes. Around us the ocean embraces us. It is the ideal mixture of hot and cold, grainy and smooth.

Every sense is deliciously occupied. Brisk sea air filters through my nose; the scent calming, and filters out my mouth; the salt tangy. The landscape is so much more fulfilling without the concealing glasses. Their strength is hiding my eyes from the world, their weakness; hiding the world from me.

We'd chosen a spot secluded from others. Though they hadn't paid us any mind. I was able to swim for the first time since last summer. The feel of silky water trailing through my hair and down my shoulders to encompass my entire body is heaven. I kick and kick. Staying under the water as long as my lungs will allow.

Twenty feet out I emerge, shaking the soaking tresses from my face and gulping in the tangy air. Invigorated, I backstroke to shore: a smile on my face so big you'd think I was the Joker.

On shore I sit with the girls. "This is amazing. Spectacular." I beam.

"Fantastic! Insane!" supplies Pinky.

Elvira adds, "Perfect."

"Yes that," I say, "Why haven't I been doing this all summer?"

"Because you're crazy—"

"Insane." They say.

Could they be right? That question swirling around in my mind I enjoy the rest of the day.

Every minute is worry free, full of bliss and laughter. My dreams find their way back to me. Prom and dating. Hope flares inside. It could happen.

The wondrous feeling follows me all the way home, where Pinky drops me off with the promise of calling later, and up the path to the front door.

Light emanates from the entry way, illuminating me like every other night. Bathed in the warm glow, I pause. A moment to myself. I feel at peace. Today was a gift. I don't want to let it go. I don't want to go inside and break the spell. But I must, so I do.

Twisting the knob, I find, much to my trepidation, the door locked. It's never locked. Not unless all four of us are behind it. Anytime of the night, if any of us were out, the knob would be waiting unlocked for someone to turn it and enter. But not tonight.

My gut twists. Discomfort settles upon me. This isn't right. Dad's way too overprotective to change this little quirk of his. Fumbling with keys is a foolish man's end. That's what he says anyways. You lose your head start in a chase that way. Paranoid is what I say.

With a heavy heart I whip out my virgin keys. Inserting the metal object I hold my breath. *Click*. Releasing the air trapped in my lungs I walk inside to see the end of every color. The end of happiness and innocence. Of rainbows and flowers and naivety. Going through the death of one set of parents is enough for a lifetime. A burden made lighter by my age. Five for Papa and seven for Mama. This, at sixteen, I can't suppress so easily.

Every step I take toward the motionless forms resounds through the silent room. I don't want to check their pulse. I don't want to check their chests for the rise and fall of functioning lungs. That would be too much. Confirmation is deadly. But I must, for Annabelle if not for me. I thank God for that one small favor; I found them and not Belle.

Pointedly ignoring Mom's shredded throat, by her own hand based on the nubs for nails – too much information, I need to breathe and focus – glazed over eyes, and gaped mouth, I lower my head to her chest.

Despite all evidence to the contrary, I hope from breath, for a pumping heart. The lack of sound sends my working heart into overdrive. Blood streams through my system quicker and quicker to keep up with my useless lungs. She's dead. *Gasp*. She'll never smile at me again or close her eyes. *Gasp*. Her spaghetti sauce won't ever again fill the house with the inviting fragrance of cinnamon. She won't hold me tight when I'm sad or sit and watch TV with me after school. *Gasp*. She's gone.

Heart breaking I crawl over to Dad. Tears blur my vision and I fall in a heap on him. Absence meets my ears again. A sob escapes me. And another as what I won't get to do with him floods me. No heart to hearts or my special birthday cake – yellow cake; in a circle not a sheet, chocolate frosting, blue sprinkles, and blue icing – no trading of sarcastic blows. No teaching me how to change a tire or walking me down the aisle. Nothing.

Just like that, in a moment of a moment, a split second, I've lost them. I've lost the people who chose me. The people who saw the best in me, who loved and nurtured me.

Composed, and the happiness before a fleeting emotion, I call Jay; my Papa's old police buddy.

Thrown back to the now I remember why I choose to forget. The future seems less daunting than the past.

Your words painted demons

and they came to life for

me. Living in my head,

strangling my heart. Though

they were your creations

they became my only

companions when you left…

Chapter 18

Shaking off the remnants of their vacant stares I pick up the walkie. "Leila checking in. Bathroom break in the works."

"Copy," comes Rudy's grainy reply.

Dylan signs in from the SUV, "Location?"

"Three hundred yards up," I answer and sign off.

"Copy."

"Copy." They both sign off.

The three of us are the impromptu leaders. Rudy of the truck. Dylan, the van. And I, the scouts.

At the clearing I park and hop off my bike. Running through the tangled mess of woods I pull out a roll of toilet paper from my trusty back pack. Don't go anywhere without it.

Unzipping my pants I prepare to pop a squat when a blur of motion catches my attention. I pause, steadying my breathing. Scanning my surroundings I wait. *There!* Near some bushes that still cling to life a

dark form emerges. It's merely a shadow.
But one made of unbridled rage.

Now that I know what's lurking I
can feel the sickly emotion pulsating off it in
waves. A Wraith. Same beast that killed my
parents.

My own rage threatens to take over
and send me charging at the wisp, but I
know better. I'd run right through it and not
a weapon in my arsenal can touch it.
Calming the boiling in my pit, I stealthily
flee. Careful for branches and dead leaves
that would give me away I slowly make my
way to the others.

Out at the edge of the road, I
frantically wave them on. All give me a look
of confusion – drooped mouths and squinted
eyes and scrunched up noses – but they ride
on. I bring my pointer finger up to my lips,
signaling silence. They obey.

Rudy, Dylan and Ezekiel move their
vehicles past the clearing and idle. The lot of
them won't continue until I've safely
mounted and started my bike.

Cautious, I don't start the engine
right away nor do I sit atop the gleaming
back frame. Instead I slide up the kick stand

carefully, quietly and start pushing my baby towards the asphalt.

Gravel slides beneath my front tire. I'm almost home free when a strong gust tips me forward and I lose my grip on the bike. Both – the bike and I – land on the unforgiving ground. Not the paint job! There's no telling how many times I've had to touch it up.

Palms down I push up using my knees as leverage. Another gust knocks me onto my side. This time I groan for me.

Clearly it's not actual wind. The Wraith has targeted me. I'm a goner. Nothing I own can dislodge it when it attacks. And based on the haze in front of me it's coming my way.

A filmy substance grips my throat like a vise. It's solid enough to turn the river of air running into my throat to a trickle. Black dots invade my vision. I can't even touch my attacker. I'm going to die without a fight.

Fear seizes hold of me and stakes its victory flag in my thudding heart. The Wraith's gaping mouth – made visible by the flow of bile colored smoke flowing from me to it – hovers above my own. It's my fear. The more fear he; the gender now made obvious by my essence, gobbles the stronger he becomes. His bony hands become fleshy and his mouth becomes solid.

Paralyzed by fear, I see smoke the color of a fresh bruise join the ranks of bile. Desperation. I know it instinctively. They go hand in hand. Fear of dying and desperation to live.

In my line of sight the Wraith materializes. He's all bones, flesh barely clinging to the yellowing substance. Each one of his ribs is easily distinguishable from the next. It's grossly obvious when he breathes; the bones pulling up and out along his lungs.

A hacking cough racks his body, sending the bones clanging. His eyes, a murky gray, latch on to mine. They change shades as I watch; a swirl of yellow and deep purple banishing the gray.

His nose-less face sniffs out the emotions whirling inside me, picking out the shiniest morsels. When all is gone he cranks it up a notch -- with the power he stole from me -- and rapes my mind; searching for what makes me tick. Having found it he starts his gruesome work.

Within seconds I feel millions of tiny legs running all over my body. Every inch. A scream dies in my throat. No sound is sufficient for what I see. Spiders. Thousands of them. Crawling over every part of me. My ears, my legs, my stomach, my hands.

Where the scream met its grave an itch begins. I open my mouth to cough but what comes out isn't phlegm. Spiders and more spiders. Creeping up my throat and exiting out my mouth. Terror takes over and I slap at every one I can reach. More acidic smoke ekes out of me.

In the distance I hear the distinct sound of a car door slamming; metal on metal. Vibrations meet my ears as feet pound their way toward me.

"Leila no!" Wails Belle.

Distraught, I flail my arms at her. She shouldn't have to die beside me. Having this monster steal every ounce of fear he can from her until her body gives out.

The Wraith hiccups at the sound of my name. My terror continues its path towards his yawning mouth but the current slows. Recognition widens the black pupils and fear erases the yellow and purple. He knows me. That's the last look I see on his face before a metal object bursts through his skull, turning him back to mist.

With the disappearance of the Wraith comes the appearance of a working trachea. Greedily, I suck in the much needed oxygen, banishing the black dots from my vision. A hand that speaks to a life of difficult work – callused, scarred, and sun chapped – reaches down to help me up. I take it without question and find myself staring into the eyes that have begun to haunt me.

"Thanks." I rasp.

He nods.

Belle runs up, with a slight limp to her step, and throws her arms around me. Tears drip on to my hair.

"Oh honey don't cry. I'm fine," I push her back to arm's length and make her look at me, "See I'm fine."

Unsure, she slowly nods.

"Let's go before it comes back," I suggest.

"Yeah." Annabelle's demeanor is still dull, subdued. A gray cloud in an otherwise clear sky.

Seeking to change the subject I turn again to Ezekiel. "Hey, so what did you use to get rid of it? Nothing we have works."

In answer he holds out what appears to be a fire poker.

"Why do you have that?"

"It's iron." He says as if it's an answer.

"And?"

The look on his face is enough to give me back my funny bone. It's like he's a cartoon character and I've said something beyond ridiculous. "Have you never seen those *Supernatural* reruns!"

"Um, I don't think so."

Here Annabelle pops in with more gusto, "Ohmygosh! The ones with the really hot brothers!?" An involuntary snort escapes me. All it takes is a hot guy to put some pep back into her step.

Ezekiel slowly says, "Sure." And changes the subject back on track, "Anyway they use iron on ghosts. Or salt."

Skeptical I point out, "Wraith's aren't ghosts."

"Looked like one."

"Yes, because ghosts can choke you." The conversation would probably go smoother without sarcasm but sometimes I can't help myself.

"Ghosts can move objects," he points out like its fact.

I growl, "I'm not an object."

Hands up in an I-surrender gesture he says, "Never said you were."

"Breathe, sis," Annabelle whispers from the side of me.

When two people give you that look that says you're no longer on the rocker it's best you back track and sit your ass on that chair. Doing as Belle suggested I calm myself and start over. "What exactly are you saying?" There's a note to my voice, an undertone of savageness that near death brings that I'm unable to suppress.

Sensing that the throes of fight still have me, Ezekiel lowers his voice to a soothing timbre. It's almost musical. Like the bass notes of a saxophone his voice is the blues, encasing me and pacifying the beast pacing just below the surface. "Perhaps the Wraith's are a sub-genre of ghosts. Ones consumed by a rage so potent they are given physical form," he has an air of a professor, as if he's teaching and not guessing, "it was just a thought." And he's back to being just as clueless as the rest of us.

"What bore the thought?" I ask, the effort of keeping myself civil causing the question to come out as a whisper.

He states simply, "What I've seen while I've been here."

I chuckle. It's that or scream. Who does this guy think he is?! What he's seen while he's been here. Seriously? I've been here a year. A whole freakin' year! And worse than that my parents were the catalyst; something I struggle to understand. But that's not the point. Ezekiel is trying to teach me about the demons that roam here like its Hell. *Me!* It's ridiculous.

Swallowing my pride I say, "I'm listening." The animal in me screams for blood. It wants to be freed to maim and mutilate. To tear the man in front of me to pieces for even thinking to teach me something.

Whether or not he doesn't see or chooses to ignore my clenched jaw and closed fists is unclear, but he continues on as if nothing's changed. "Around the time I first dropped down there was a woman. She was wailing and crying so loud I had to cover my ears. It echoed off the buildings and filled every inch of the air. I thought to go to her, to see if I could help. But the closer I got I noticed she wasn't all there."

"Obviously," interjects Annabelle, "she was making a shitload of noise in a hellion infested area. Can you say stupid?"

"Language," I say. She gives me a whatever look and turns back to Ezekiel.

"That's not what I mean by all there. But duh, yeah she was crazy. But she was spectral too. I could see through her."

"So she's a ghost. So what." I'm ready to dismiss all this speculation and feel the open road beneath me again. The need to roam is overwhelming.

Frustration causes him to roll his eyes. "Yeah, she's a ghost but it's more than that. When I got closer I noticed a man leaning against the side of a building. He was bawling his eyes out. Like snot and hiccupping and everything. I saw the same stuff that was seeping out of you seep out of him."

Attention caught, I press for more. "What color was it?"

"A deep navy blue tinged with black. At first I thought it odd. I had to be seeing things. But then I started to feel it." Tremors move through him as he shakes off the memory.

"Feel what?" I ask.

"This, this like," he slides his fingers into his unruly hair and grips tight, grasping for the right words, "despair. It was grief and sorrow and despair all in one pressing on me like a weight."

Annabelle is as captivated as me. "That sounds terrible."

"It was, but there's more."

He seems hesitant to continue and the beast in me softens, "She's not here."

Ezekiel blows out a breath and starts, "The wails turned into music. It was the most melancholy sound; plucking at me soul and stealing happiness, but music nonetheless. I didn't know what to make of it, but I knew if I stayed I'd end up like that guy."

"Bean Sidhe?" I whisper to myself. Not possible.

"What are you whispering about, sis?"

"Nothing, Belle." I can't even talk right now. A Bean Sidhe in San Jose. That's not even a demon. And this isn't Ireland.

In my mind a battle ensues. Calculated logic vs. frenzied fear. If the scope of monsters around here expands to twisted versions on non-demons then we are totally screwed.

It couldn't be a Bean Sidhe. They wail for the dead not wail them to death. Perhaps it's just as Ezekiel said: spirits consumed by such a strong, dreadful emotion are given form and continue to wreak havoc on the living.

A nasty thought seeps into my brain. The implications of Ezekiel's theory being right hits too close to home. I'd always suspected a Wraith, but now to know the motive behind the creature's movements is almost too much. But it's the most plausible explanation.

Grudgingly, I give in, "You may be on to something." In Leila language that's telling him he's right. He might not know that, but based on the look on my little sister's face she does.

"Wipe that smirk off your face, Belle."

"What smirk?" she asks angelically. Yeah, she has a halo alright…held up by horns.

I punch her in the arm, playfully of course, any more force than necessary is a total accident, and reach down to lift up my bike.

My injured sister steps in to help me. "What are you doing?"

"Helping you," she replies firmly.

"I'm fine."

"No, you're not. You have a necklace of bruises and you look pale."

"So what? You almost died and you're walking around." Ezekiel is smart enough to stay out of it. He stands at ease and waits for the family duel to die down.

"Leila, please stop being difficult," pleads Annabelle.

My beast shakes at its cage. "Not now, Belle."

She does the exact opposite of what I need; bears down and digs in. "You're hurt. Liath can take the bike and you can ride in the SUV."

The beast howls its distaste. The open road, air in my face, it's what I want. What I need. Every time the blood lust comes it's what I do. Irritation takes hold? I take off. Rage boils up; air simmers it down. And when that doesn't work killing demons does. I need freedom. "No," I snarl.

Damn it to the sacredness of family feuds, Ezekiel maneuvers his body between the stunned Belle and my rigid form. "How about a compromise?" he suggests.

Belle shrugs. I remain still. "Leila keeps her bike, but I take point." My first instinct is to snarl, but one look at his pleading eyes and the sound dies in my throat. He's saving me, not Annabelle.

"Sure. Whatever," agrees Belle, a wounded look in her eyes, but right now I'm incapable of caring.

I should be grateful to Ezekiel, but even that is an emotion that eludes me. The only feeling firmly in place is fear. Even with the Wraith gone it continues to consume me.

Annabelle gives me one last indecipherable look before turning and walking away. Her steps are heavy, a slow that is caused by defeat. A twinge of something attacks my heart but before long terror gobbles it up.

My anger was a pulsing creature inside.

It was its own entity. Living to make

my life hell.

Chapter 19

At first Ezekiel stays true to his word and takes point. But the beast, not completely quelled, demands I shake off the shackles. Biding my time I wait for the right moment, when Annabelle's worried face can no longer peer at me through the dirty windshield.

When the time comes I ramp up the speed. Rapidly, I gain on Ezekiel and pass him within seconds. But I don't slow, even though he makes no move to surpass me. The wind rips through my hair like greedy fingers. Dust pelts all exposed skin, turning me three shades darker. For me this is release.

Sometimes though it's just not enough. Rage slides over my eyes and I see red. The hum of Ezekiel's pursuit keeps the rage in place. My heart beats to the fury of the wind. The blood running through my veins boils as hot as the gas sending me forward.

When I'm in this state every intellectual part of me is stripped to its core. Animal instinct rules and I'm a slave to it.

Winds greedy fingers grab hold of my consciousness and I become all monster.

It's the monster that commits the next atrocious acts. Even as I scream at it to subdue, only to subdue, it doesn't listen.

I see the line of nails too late. The front tire explodes on impact and I lose control. Sparks fly where metal meets gravel. Blood spills where skin meets concrete.

Barely coming to a halt, I'm met by three attackers. They converge on me like a wave on sandy shores. Their scent invades my nose and makes me gag. They pin me down and go straight for my pants. I lay still. Still as death. They don't need to know they've made the worst mistake of their short lives.

Thinking I'm giving in, that I'm not dangerous, the balding one and the toothless one go about searching my bike. The idiots quickly dismiss the crossbow that was ripped from me during my dramatic descent to the unforgiving ground. My bleeding arm, sparsely furnished with pebbles, cries out in pain at the reminder.

Quickly, I hide the weakness. My adversaries could use it against me; though I don't think them smart enough. Two of them are stuffing their faces with what provisions I have while the other is salivating and eating me with his eyes. I know what he intends for me. He is like so many others I've dispatched. All I have to do is wait, remain calm and take the first opportunity that affords me the upper hand.

The opportunity presents itself when he goes frantically to work on his belt, his beady eyes never leaving my breasts. Without a second thought, I wiggle my legs free from beneath his weight and latch them like a leech to his beefy neck. Squeezing as tightly as I can I wait for the tell-tale collapse of the windpipe.

His audacity begs me to make him suffer. Hot blood sings to me a tune of his slow demise. I let his oxygen supply fade, bit by bit. He's suffocating. Once he begins to turn a dangerous shade of purple, a sharp pivot of my hips ends it all. Number 22 dead of a broken neck. Against the monster's wishes I decide 23 and 24 won't suffer.

Once they realize their buddy is dead and gone they scramble to their feet. I'm now a threat. On my way up to face them I grab both hunting knifes from my boots. The ones I hastily restocked after our run in with the demons.

Toothless or rather 23 comes at me with a lethal looking blade: serrated edges and mat black finish, but his grip is too tight. He can't roll with the punches, flow with the fight and I disarm him effortlessly, slicing his Achilles tendon as I go. He is now useless. Like he thought me.

Before I can finish him off Baldy tackles me to the ground. He surprises me. I'll give him that, but his posture is sloppy and I shake him loose as we go down. 24 lands harder than I, jarring him to the bone.

He isn't quick to recover so I deal with his buddy: steel slides against flesh and it's lights out. My free hand throws the second blade without hesitation. With it the monster wins: no survivors. In a moment 24 is like the incubi, blood pouring out his chest. 23's already dry. Severing the carotid will do that.

During the whole ordeal I tell myself its necessary. Now that the red has faded from my eyes and moved to stain my hands I say its kill or be killed. That wasn't the beast. Letting them live was problematic.

But it isn't that simple. Not when I have a captive audience and I know my attackers were simply starved and crazed and I'm...well I'm the true monster.

I look up, crimson splashed across my face, drops of blood dripping from my gory hands to the sleek pavement below and see them. Awe and horror mingle on their faces. They don't need to put in to words what I can already see; they're afraid of me.

Dazed and horrified I drop my blades and fall to my knees. Blood splashes up, soaking my jeans further and steel clangs. Acidic bile rises in my stomach. Puke fills my mouth. I push it back down.

Noise is fuzzy. Doors open and yells sound, but their muffled. Footsteps slap the wet pavement, the pavement doused in blood, but instead of lumbering boots I hear ballet slippers.

Rage slips away, back into the pit, but red remains. It's everywhere. Streaking the sky. Drowning the pavement. Staining my cloths. Marring my hands. I'm in an ocean of crimson. The monster hiding beneath the froth surfacing only when hunger strikes. Satiated, my consciousness returns. I. Did. This.

Liquid bubbles up inside and finds escaped through eyes. Shamelessly I cry, allowing the salty tears to wash away my sins. 24 humans weigh on my shoulders. Their outrage breaks me. I'm an earthquake, inundated with regret. Bedeviled by guilt I attempt to hide my face. Only to be stopped short by my murderous hands.

Kenzie kneels before me, the terror carefully hidden from her features. She's talking but I can't hear her. The dead are too loud. Asking me why. Why did I slit their throat? Why did I snap their neck? I can't answer them. Nothing excuses it. I can't tell them it wasn't me, it was the beast. The beast is me. I am the beast.

"Leila, Leila, honey, look at me," Kenzie says.

"Can't." I croak. Stained hands capture my attention. It's like the time in middle school art class when we got to work with the pottery wheel. Except the caked up color in the creases of my palms is more sinister. These hands just killed three men. Three starving men.

Her hands grab my face and I jerk away. There's blood tainting my features. I don't want my sin on her, but she's persistent.

"Look. At. Me."

Quelled, I do. "It's okay. You did what you had to."

Still unable to speak I employ my eyes to express my torment. She picks up the sign easily. God bless her. "I know baby. I know," it seems repetition is a calming device, "but they would've killed you."

"Subdue," I manage, my eyes downcast in shame.

"He was going to rape you. I saw. I would've killed him too." Lies. Mackenzie is too pure for death. She would've choked him out, not viciously snapped his neck. She's anger-less. All good. I don't tell her that though.

Shocked and ill, I'm pliable and Kenzie easily drags me to my unsteady feet. Someone, Dylan based on the streak of black that invades my vision, hands her a damp cloth. Gingerly she uses it to erase the evidence of my heinous acts from my face. Next, she goes about purifying my murderous hands. In moments the crime has been eradicated from my person. No bystander would stop and think that the three bodies on the ground are my doing.

A sigh of relief escapes me as I'm herded into Rudy's truck like cattle. I've managed to avoid Belle a little longer. What she must think of me sends my stomach churning. For her to fear me, for any of them to fear me breaks my spirit.

Like a hermit crab I retreat into my shell where every noise is muffled, every sight is blurred like I'm submerged in water. The silky substance takes me to another world where shock rules and horror lurks.

No one tells you the ugly parts about love.
The parts where you're lying in bed,
screaming into a pillow and begging God to
make the hurt stop. They don't tell you the
pain it causes. That it feels like you're
being torn apart from the inside. What it is
to wake up with puffy eyes: evidence of all
the tears you've cried. Conveniently, they
neglect to mention what it's like to walk
around a shadow of yourself. To know
there's
something vital missing but being unable to
explain it or get it back. Not a soul mentions
the most hideous part of love – when it ends.

Chapter 20

For the duration of the day I remain in my shell. While I'm aware of the goings on, they don't penetrate. For hours I neither eat or speak. The back seat of Rudy's truck becomes my home. Curled up I steep in self-hatred.

Only when Mr. Sun creeps towards the horizon do I stir. Shell broken by the onset of night I have no choice but to rise from the fetal position. Mechanically, I shake myself back into reality and speak for the first time since the slaughtering.

Having not been used for the entirety of the day my vocal cords protest. Clearing my throat loosens them nicely. "Stop up there."

Rudy's training is so engrained in him that he doesn't so much as flinch. He merely follows orders and pulls in front of the house. "Why here?"

"Because it'll be the only house for another few miles and while the roads are fairly clear and the demons sparse there's no telling if that'll change." Even checked out I notice what's important to the group's survival. I've added three bodies to my shoulders today; I have no intention of adding any more.

I'm the first one on the ground and heading to the door before the rest know what's up. In the background static signals Rudy informing the others. To my liking the door is locked. Right now, in the present it's a great sign. If there's anyone still inside they're likely sane and if not we will move on. No more blood will coat my hands tonight.

Everything about the house speaks to life; human life and a lack of demons. No boards over the windows. The porch light signs like a beckon, a bright soul in a world of darkness. But still there's something that bothers me. A piece of the puzzle missing. Something off putting that tells the bypasser this is no longer a safe haven. Perhaps it's the absence of noise at 5:30 in the evening.

A life of civilization spurs me to knock anyway. Precious seconds lost to the act. No one answers. A sinking feeling starts somewhere in my abdomen. It could be nothing, but it feels like *something*.

Waiting for the others is crucial. An unspoken rule we all follow. It's what I'm supposed to do. It prevents loss of life, but for that reasoning I kick open the door. Before the door can slam shut I shoulder my way in.

The putrid smell of rotting flesh is nowhere to be found. A blessing really, but still my heart is hammering. Despite a lack of evidence pointing to a struggle and the fact that there are no bodies to been seen or smelled I feel like I've walked into a nightmare.

I can hear the others behind me, but anticipation tethers me to the labyrinth of halls and stairs before me. Following the pull I make my way up the stairs. At the top a door faces me, but it's not the one I'm searching for and so I turn left. Chest ready to burst I push open the cracked door. Deep inside I know what I face will destroy me. Every nerve in my body screams at me to turn around. My very bones want to flee. But my heart, that infernal organ that keeps me alive, insists I cross the threshold. So I do.

Nothing in my short life could've prepared me for what I now face. No amount of blood, bodies, or battles could've shattered my being as effectively as this room has. The rocking chair in the corner is

far more sinister than blood-stained walls.
The stack of toys in the corner affects me
more than any pile of bodies ever has. And
when I turn towards the antique crib every
hardship I've ever encountered pales in
comparison. Even stanching Belle's
bleeding was easier than forcing myself to
step forward.

Voices rise in the background as the
others find what is sure to be the parent's
bodies. But I only have eyes for the little
angel laying still in the crib bellow. There's
not a hair out of place on her head and a
flush of pink tickles her chubby cheeks. To
all who look she appears alive. But on closer
inspection one can see that her lungs aren't
pumping oxygen to her tiny body.

Grief crashes over me. More intense
than I've ever felt before. Knees buckling I
collapse. Grasping the slates of the crib I
stare at the baby girl. She's beautiful. A
bright spot in a world of darkness, but her
soul has dimmed and faded. She's gone too
soon.

Despair dances around my heart with
her partner guilt. I could've saved her. If
we'd gotten here moments earlier those
long, dark eyelashes that kiss her pinch-able
cheeks could flutter and lift. If I hadn't

fought the tether that bound me to her, if I hadn't hesitated or sought a way out perhaps right now she'd be gazing into my eyes. But ifs aren't reality.

Pulling myself together; wiping the tears from my eyes and slowing my anxious heart, I call to the others. From their expressions I gather my Intel. Both parents dead. No obvious cause though as with my little angel. I don't know when I claimed her, but it feels right.

"Liath, Dylan, I need you to dig graves."

Oblivious to the turmoil raging inside me Liath states, "We don't bury the dead." As with waiting for the others before a breach it's an unspoken rule. For many reason really. First and foremost: it's a waste of time. No matter how quickly we dig more will always pile up. Number two: the stench of rotting corpses hides the scent of our very live and for many demons very delicious flesh. And finally, in a pinch they make a workable barricade. I'm not proud of the last, but to survive one has to let go of certain beliefs about humanity; like respecting the dead.

Quietly, I say, "Today we do." Blue eyes flicker to closed ones. How I wish I knew her eye color. To look into the windows to the soul and not find an empty home. Papa always used to say "if wishes were fishes". He'd never finish the rhythm, hell that might be the whole thing, but if wishes were fishes I'd pick up a pole right now.

"How many?" Dylan asks stoically.

"Two."

"But—" I cut him off. I know what he'll say.

"I'll dig the third." No one questions me, however Ezekiel comes up and lays a hand on my arm. The gesture is welcome and I allow myself the weakness.

"Thank you." He nods and I get to work.

At the door I pause, a nagging in my pit, "Will you stay with her?" "

"Consider me her guardian angel." Tears prick my eyes as I close the door; the others having already left to fulfill out their perspective duties, I'm starting to really like this guy. Respect him.

Everything in me wants to fall to pieces, to slide down to the floor, bring my knees to my chest and let go of control. But now's not the time. My little angel deserves a proper burial. And I'll give it to her.

Outside I'm amazed by what I see. This family was completely self-sustaining. A vegetable garden takes up half the yard, while fruit trees populate any space they can. A water collection system sits in a corner. I'm guessing they were Preppers. It didn't save them. Though who knows what killed them. Had the creature never showed up, this little plot of land would've kept them alive for quite some time. And judging by the vibrancy of the produce, what a life it would've been.

The guys have found a lovely plot of land under a towering apple tree. Joining them I pick up a shovel and dig. Once the hole is a good three feet deep – no shallow grave for my little angel – and three feet long by two feet wide I stand and stretch. Behind the horizon the sun now hides and my friend ,the moon, has taken her throne in the sky.

Three graves; a tiny one nestled between two larger, paints a picture of misery. High on her throne the moon mourns with us; basking the haunting scene in her pale light. Above the graves – two filled and covered – the apple trees bare branches hovers over in protection. Noise erupts in an otherwise silent night. Crickets playing their music and a few birds signing their song. It's a goodbye.

It's well beyond witching hour when I finally make my way back towards the illuminated house. The descent up the stairs is difficult. Each step looms larger than life. The banister sways under my sweaty palms. As much as I don't want to do this; even the mere idea of covering the precious baby laying in that crib makes me want to puke, for her I must.

Reminding myself I'm just burying a body doesn't help. Having reached adolescents in a household where God mattered I'd been taught that in the end the body lays empty. Everything important has fled to its true final resting place. But that's no comfort now. Not now when I have a child-sized hole to fill.

I'm facing her door before I'm ready. I suppose I'd never be ready though. How does one prepare for something like this? I yearn to know her name, to know her smile and giggle. Even to hear her cry, but I refuse to paw through this family's belongings. Here everything is different. Perhaps it's the knowledge that I could've saved them. Should've saved them. Guilt's a funny emotions like that; connecting you to someone in ways unimagined.

Maybe it's not even guilt, though it feels like it. Maybe it's curiosity. Their lack of flesh wounds or an obvious cause of death nags at me. At the others as well. It's as if their souls just up and left. It doesn't make any sense. Whatever the reason the connection is there and no amount of stalling will make it go away.

And so I enter her room for the last time. Ezekiel leans by the crib, a book in his hand: *Love You Forever*. He's reading to her, "I'll love you forever, I'll like you for always, as long as I'm living my baby you'll be." My Mama used to read that book to me. It sat on my night stand tattered and faded from use. It's the perfect send off for my little angel.

I don't want to disturb them. I don't want to take her away. Right now, with him reading to her like she can still listen I can feel her presence. Picking her up, wrapping her in a blanket and leaving the room will break the spell.

But as with all things I'd rather not do, I do them anyway. "Hey."

"Hey," he lamely holds up the children's book, "I was just reading her a story."

"I can see that," I say.

"I guess you can."

"Yeah." Standing here my heart is breaking. Not crying is impossible. Tears slid down my cheeks and for once I let them. "It's time."

Ezekiel is crying also. I guess he's claimed her too. "Would you like me to carry her?"

I would, but my heart doesn't. This is my job, my responsibility. "No, thank you. But would you follow me and bring the bear." In her crib there's one stuffed animal – a white bear with a pink beanie – sitting by itself. Its eyes are brown,

"Of, course." He sets down the book and my heart slams against my rib cage.

"Don't leave the book." Relief crosses his features. So I'm not crazy; at least where this ordeal is concerned.

Finally, the times come and I'm looking down at my little angel. Picking her up seals it. There's only one place she's going. With great pains I lean over, the crib biting into my stomach, and lift her up. Having been secured with great measure and love, the blanket that cradles her stays put. It's a pale yellow and is striking against her dark hair. Even as young as she is, probably no more than five months, she has a head full of curls. The pink of her cheeks have long faded. Truly she is dead to the world.

I ask of Ezekiel one last thing before departing. "Please find another blanket. Something pretty I can cover her with." That it will be a shroud is unspoken. Though we know I'm carrying her to her funeral, we don't speak of it. Voicing it is more than we can take.

With lead weighing me down I make my descent down the stairs, cross the threshold between indoors and out, and walk to the empty grave. Hope has me searching one last time for life, but nothing. Choking on sobs I kneel in the dirt. Shaking hands run through her curls and trail down her face. It's so cold. Tears drip onto her cherub-like face as I lean down to kiss her forehead. The heat of my body refuses to penetrate. She's past the point of help.

Having kneeled beside me, Ezekiel gives her his own farewell kiss. Our tears mingle and slip down the sides, mimicking her own. "Goodbye," he whispers, a crack in his voice. He doesn't leave though. Through everything he stays by my side.

While repeating my favorite line from *Love You Forever* I lay her in the dirt, "I'll love you forever, I'll like you for always, As long as I'm living my baby you'll be." I choke on the last line, the words coming out broken and strained.

Wordlessly, Ezekiel hands me a crocheted blanket. Obviously homemade it's perfect. All pastel colors and soft fabric. Silently I lay it over her, taking in her features one last time before covering her face. Ezekiel nestles the bear into her side, forever hugging her. All that can be done is done. Now the soul shattering begins.

Quaking with held in pain I shovel dirt in. Scoop by scoop I fill the hole. The entire time my stomach is churning and my chest burning, but I don't let Ezekiel take over. I need to do this. For her. Filled and smooth, my little angel's grave is the opposite of my insides; missing pieces and cratered.

Death holds me firmly

in his grasp

--like a lover.

Life courses through

my veins, but he whispers

to my heart.

Promising to embrace me

and steal away the pain those

living are blind to.

Chapter 21

I lay there for a while, by her grave, careless of the dirt covering me. No one bothers me, not even my silent guard: Ezekiel. Hours have passed since my sobs turned to silent tears. These; however, don't change. Even as the Moon retires for the day and the Sun glides towards his reign I continue to cry.

Finally, noises penetrate the fog I'm lost in. The gang's awake. We will be leaving soon. One more day of riding and we should reach our destination. A mixture of bitterness and relief attacks me. I don't want to go ask "mommy" and "daddy" for help, but I'm done with this road trip. Too much has happened in so little time.

Worry needles its way into the mixture. I'll have a lot to chew on and questions to have answered once the others are safe. What the answers will be, I don't know, but I fear them. What my biological parents could know of my ancestry and if that ancestry could intersect with less than human descendants is something I need to know. Being under the water for over an hour, not breathing is not normal. Having demons searching for me is not normal.

Especially because their intent doesn't seem malicious. Something is going on, that much I'm sure of, but whether that something will end with me in a strait jacket is yet to be determined.

But for now I have other things to focus on. After a night of being curled up on the dirt I'm stiff and tired. My eyes are puffy and cheeks chapped. I'm filthy; dirt covering every available inch.

"Why don't you go take a shower and get something to eat?" Ezekiel. So he speaks.

"I'm not hungry." But the shower sounds nice so I push myself to my feet.

The beauty of spending a year with a select group of people is that they learn your tells. No words need to be spoken for a point to be made or feelings to be shared. Everything from their gestures to their tone of voice is second nature to me, as is mine for them. We knew each other in and out.

Today that is my saving grace. During the night a bond forged between Ezekiel and me. It's lost on no one. Of their own accord Rudy and Ezekiel switch places: Ezekiel now owns the truck and Rudy the remaining bike. This allows me to stay where I feel safe, surprisingly by the newcomer's side.

No one speaks to me as I make my way inside and follow the path towards the downstairs bathroom. Empty, I enter and undress. The water feels amazing on my skin; washing away last night's sorrow. An ache remains, but it's bearable and beneath the surface. Clean I emerge to find fresh clothes stacked on the toilet. Mackenzie. Her motherly touches never go unrecognized or unappreciated. Parentless, the lot of us, it helps to have someone do the little things a mom or dad would usually do. A fresh set of jeans and shirt do wonders for my mood. I feel like a new person; less like someone who buried a baby recently.

Everyone is ready when I get out and waiting in the vehicles. Others might see this –not helping pack up the vehicles or even having breakfast with the gang-- as rude, but this is their way of showing me love. Eyes on me make me uncomfortable. I can't deal. It makes me sweat and feel cagey.

I hop into the truck, taking the passenger seat over the back this time. On the dash lays *Love You Forever*. Studiously, I ignore it. I've moved past last night...for now at least. The gang needs my head in the game. A day longer of driving, tops, and we will arrive at our destination. Ahead of schedule. Then is when I can truly look back at the events of the past night. Look back at the emotions tightly contained behind my wall.

The day passes in a blur. Uneventful. ACDC and Led Zepplin blare from the radio. I guess Ezekiel likes the oldies. He doesn't press me to talk but every now and then he'll reach over and squeeze my hand. Every time I hold my breath and hope he won't let go. But he does.

Our relationship is an odd one. Something I don't want but crave. To have attention after a year of being the "extra" is invigorating. It seems like more than that though. Even before last night there was something more. A connection that scared me into suspicion.

Trying not to dwell on all the emotions heaving themselves at my wall is difficult. Over the past few days I've been tested in ways I didn't know possible. Discoveries have been made that only lead to more questions. What has once been my nightmare – meeting the Biologicals – has become my only salvation. They hold the answers to my strange questions. Questions that every day become more necessary to answer.

Crooked, barely upright on the side of the road a sign reads "Welcome to Oregon!". We are almost there. A few more hours, five at most, and I will be facing one of my greatest fears. All other questions and thoughts flee from my mind and into the abyss. They can't compete with a lifetimes worth of worry.

Straightening in my seat I prepare for the last leg of the race. We should be stopping for lunch sometime soon and then one last stretch, providing there are no bathroom breaks. One weak bladder means we all get held up. No one gets left behind.

As I suspected the request for lunch comes in on the walkie. "Mackenzie. Lunch break?"

Short, sweet and simple. Name and question.

Rudy answers, of course in the affirmative because it's his girl. "Yes. Stop about two miles ahead."

"Copy."

Ezekiel follows suit. "Copy." And then he turns and offers me a slice of heaven. "You want to ditch the others?"

"We can't." Comes my immediate response. Damn Rudy and all his lectures. What he says truly does penetrate my thick skull. No matter what he might think.

The sexy man to my right chuckles. Alone the noise is capable of traveling through me, seeking out all the hidden nooks and crannies and banishing the dark. Light reigns where the sound touches. Weight dispels from my heart. I am a feather. His laugh is a drug flowing through my veins. I'm high on it.

"What I meant was we can have lunch just the two of us. Some place close to the others, but not to close. Sound good?'

Riding the high, I say yes without hesitation.

We pass the others and keep rolling. They just wave and turn their attention back to their food. Despite the amount of food we brought we are always hungry. There is no mindless snacking on the road or really any snacking. Preserves are just in case food. Just in case we can't find food. Just in case we get lost. Just in case our destination turns out to be a bust.

With the weather being agreeable and the dust profoundly less invasive the further north we drive, Ezekiel and I choose to eat outside of the truck. Leaning against a tree I find the bark to be rough but not bothersome. The dirt is hard packed and slightly frozen through in some areas but I can't find it in me to care about the uncomfortable state of my seating arrangements. I'm in a state of mind that neglects all outside sensations.

It's not so much that I don't notice them, that I'm so consumed with inner thoughts that the outside matters not. It's more along the lines that I've resolved not to care. Introverted I can handle what comes next. If I allow all that goes on outside my body to invade then my carefully controlled emotions will escape. With my ribs as the only defense between the world and all its soul breaking qualities and my heart, it's a precarious situation. And right now I can't afford to loosen the noose.

Ezekiel having grown in tuned to my needs and emotions through the night simply hands me a beef stick and some dried fruit: peaches and bananas this time. To have one piece of fresh, right off the vine anything would be incredible. The thought makes my mouth water and my stomach growl. We could've plundered my little angel's garden but that felt wrong. Like invading Eden.

Mr. Sarcasm mistakes the whale like noises emitting from my stomach to be hunger. "Stop staring at your food and eat. It'll help with the rumbling."

Rather than explain to him my want of fresh food I stick my tongue out and dramatically tear off a piece from the beef stick. For my benefit I'm sure, he remains silent. All is not quiet though. Fallen leaves scrap across the road and rustle on the grass that clings to life. In the wind branches creak and groan. Gnashing teeth join the symphony as we work our way through the tough meat. The mixture of sounds is oddly peaceful and I find myself relaxing. My deadly emotions remain where they must but my thoughts are free to wander without fear because how, with a scene like this before me, can one think poisonous thoughts?

By now I should know that peaceful moments are rare and seldom last long. Today calm shatters at the presence of a strange man. Nothing about him marks him as either Deranged or Starved. His appearance if that of someone well fed, as well as can be expected in troubled times, and recently bathed. Teeth do not rot in his mouth and rags hang not from his limbs. He is simply a man. One you might see on the streets back in the Before.

Cautiously, he approaches. The whole while staring at me as if I'm a specimen. Though his gaze differs from that of the hellions: he doesn't see me as one of his own. I'm a puzzle he is trying to solve.

A split second changes everything. His calm demeanor slips away like a second skin and before me he turns into a Deranged. It starts with a quiet whisper. One word: Temptress.

Were emotional abuse

visible

If the wounds seeped

blood

The way those inflicted

on the body do

She'd be nothing more

than scar tissue.

Chapter 22

Steadily his insult rises in pitch. "Temptress, Temptress, TEMPTRESS!!" Now, at the top of his lungs he screams. Other vile words join the mix: demon, seductress, whore. With each accusation comes a step forward.

Transfixed by the escalation transpiring in front of me, I don't move. I watch as he makes his way towards me. Spittle flying and eyes burning. Ezekiel, on the other hand, rises gradually. Mere moments ago he was smiling, his limbs were lax and his voice soothing. He has now become my protector.

"Sir, you need to stop right there."

Unfazed the man continues forward. "Whore. Demon. Two-faced!" The last one's new and questionable. It doesn't fit with the others. Another odd puzzle piece.

The mad man before me does not notice the tower rising to his left. Nor does he seem to care. "Lies, lies, lies. Your face lies!" Distressed he covers his eyes. However, no matter the terror my face causes him he can't help but peek. His infatuation is like the men in the Before. Only he seems aware of the trickery. If it can even be called that.

Like a human shield Ezekiel stands between the advancing man and me. Unperturbed by the sudden obstacle in his way he simply side steps him and attempts to reach me. Beneath Ezekiel's shirt his muscles bunch. A coil about to spring, he's ready to take him down. Not wanting anymore blood spilled today; for once sickened by its coppery scent, I speak. "Sir?"

My voice is a pause button. Half way through his step he falters. His foot just sort of hangs mid-air before falling beneath gravity's weight. As he's called me a demon I figure my smartest and safest route is to define myself as human. "I am human. My names Leila and I'm just trying to get home to my parents." The sentence is sand paper in my throat, but keeping this stranger alive is worth the discomfort.

Still, he stands and contemplates my words. It looks, for a moment, like he believes me or wants to believe me. But I witness the gate shutting on his feelings. He will not be swayed by my face, by my words, or by my actions. There is nothing I can say that will change his mind. Action is all that's left.

With strength born of determination, he shoves Ezekiel in the chest and knocks him to his ass. Stunned, Ezekiel is helpless to stop what comes next. With tears pooling in his eyes the stranger falls on top of me. From thin air he produces a blade and holds it to my throat. "You're wrong. All wrong." His words hitch as he cries. It's clear to me he's struggling. I'll more than likely be his first kill for I will shed no more blood today.

Though instinct tells me to close my eyes, to look away from Death I do not. The murmurings of a mad man have me in their thrall. "Wrong! Not what I want. No. No. No. Your face is wrong."

As he speaks he shakes-- miniature convulsions. Each brings the blade closer to my neck. And still I watch him and wait. The balls in his court so to speak. I won't fight back. If blood shall be spilled today it'll be my own.

His internal battle reaches its apex as he begins to have a conversation with himself. "Just a girl. She's just a girl. Human. Says she's human. But no. Look at her, those eyes, that face. No. No. More, she's more. But wrong. All wrong. Face is wrong."

I swallow, causing the blade to nick my throat; it stings, a reminder of the danger I'm facing, and prepare my defense. One last ditch effort to prevent all bloodshed. "I'm not more, sir. Simply a lost girl looking for her parents. The eyes," mentioning them gets his full attention, "are my mothers."

"Your mothers?"

"Yes." The man wavers. Steel slips to the side, drawing more blood but the pressure is released. I quiet my heart and press on. Perhaps there is hope after all. "And the face--"

"Yes. Wrong." Agitated once more he brings the blade back to its originally position. Fear has me reaching for sarcasm, "--good genes and all."

"It's not right! " He shrieks. Spit flies and hits me in the face. "Not what I desire. It's not."

Slowly, I begin to realize the heart of his problem. The puzzle pieces move together to create a picture. He believes me to be a succubus. And apparently the face he's seeing --mine-- isn't what he most desires and that's causing him to become extremely distressed.

"I'm no succubus." My declaration comes out harsher than I intend. But with all the questions concerning my true ancestry I'm a little touchy about the subject.

However, it's a stupid mistake that cost me any chance of convincing this man I'm human. He takes my anger as a sign that I'm caught in a lie. "You are. Liar! You'll die. Like my wife died."

His arm tenses as my body does. He's readying for the final blow. A little more pressure and a swift movement to the side and not only will my air way be cut in half but my carotid will be sliced open. As the blood flows out of me I'll become cold and calm. With no blood in me there will be no room for panic. Just sweet release and the knowledge that my sacrifice will have saved this man.

Determined to meet Death with eyes open I fixate my eyes on the mad man in front of me. He, on the other hand, does all he can to keep from looking at me. Those brown eyes of his shine with unshed tears.

This strange man might believe me to be a monster but he is no killer. Proof of his clean hands is present in the way he shakes and avoids eye contact.

Killing me will scar him, change him in ways only murder can, but he will be alive. Nerves overtake me. I don't want to die. I muster two words, "it's okay." Finally his eyes find me, tears have since spilled over and make tracks down his ruddy cheeks.

Risking further injury from the steel pressed to my throat I nod. More blood spills. The warm liquid slides down my throat and drips to the ground below. Soon the earth will bathe in blood. It will scream its rage at another pointless death. The moon will weep at another child lost and the sun with dry the evidence of yet another horror. And I'll be free.

Ezekiel has another plan in mind. Transfixed by my face the man atop me fails to notice the sudden loss of sunlight. As the shadow falls over us Ezekiel springs forward and fastens his bulky arms around the man's throat.

Torn from me the strange man struggles for his life. My body rushes to catch up with my mind so I can beg Ezekiel to let him live. It's not happening fast enough. I'm speechless. Having prepared myself for death I'm in another place.

Paralyzed for the moment, all I can decipher is a tangled mess of limbs. It's unclear who is who as they continue to scramble about. Eventually Ezekiel rises and my mind and heart fight each other. Done with bloodshed my heart slams into my rib change, praying the strange man is still alive. Thinking of survival my mind is satisfied that death now no longer awaits me.

But as is typical my heart overrules my mind and I begin to yell at him. "No! It should've been me. I was ready! Damn you."

On my feet now I advance and push him. The bastard doesn't budge. Furious I pound at his chest: soft flesh bouncing off a solid surface. Quietly, he allows my outburst. When I've expended all my energy he firmly grabs my face and makes me look at him. "He's not dead."

The sentence is foreign. It's the last combination of words I expected to fall from his mouth. For a second in time I mirror the strange man: I've been paused. All I can do is stare at the tower before me and stand in awe of his restraint. He did what I've never been capable of: only subdue . And I was witness to his face; the anger contained there was a deadly force. And yet no one died.

Ashamed I mumble a half ass apology and walk away. A bird in the sky, my happiness flies away. "Let's go."

Fed up with being weak, fragile

she retreated from the world

and in doing so encased her heart in ice

Quickly it overtook her

until her arms, legs, head

her very veins pulsed with the frozen liquid

Feelings fled and she was left emotionless

pain could no longer touch her

And grief? A long ago nightmare

But she did not think of everything –

Removed from the world of emotions

she too lost its beauty

Happiness could not enter her heart

peace was merely a dream

And love? Could not penetrate her cold exterior.

Chapter 23

It's time. There's no demons to deter us or mad men lurking in dark corners. We've made it to Caelo.

The town is small. We make it through it and on to its outskirts in under forty five minutes. I don't pay attention to much though a couple of help wanted signs attract my attention. Here I will most certainly pull my own weight and I expect the same of the others.

Ezekiel pulls over to the curb and the others follow his lead. We're here. The Biological's. "Are you ready?" he asks.

No. Hell no! I could never be ready for this. I never even wanted this. And now they hold more than my DNA inside them, more than a what my life could've been, more than what it would've been like to never have been an orphan. They hold all the answers I crave so vehemently. But yes is all I say.

A deep breath settles my mind and allows me to step outside the vehicle. Any calm it might've given me shatters at the view in front of me. Their estate is sprawling. Two stories high and buttressed against the ocean. Wisteria climbs up lattices to the second story windows. Two cars sit polished and clean in the carved stone driveway.

Water-efficient landscaping sits beside the greenest lawn you've ever seen. The grass goes on for about half a soccer field before it ends at their Redwood deck. Up the deck one meets an entry way made for a giant. Double doors eight feet high with knockers made of brass.

For a moment a fury fills me like no other. I hate them and their damn money. I hate their beautiful house and perfect cars. I hate that they have no fence because they feel safe. Safe! What I would give to feel safe. I hate that they gave me up so they could have all this.

Seeing all they have, a beach front property and a comfortable life, puts a price on me. Had they kept me would they still have all this? Was I not enough? How I would've loved them. But they never gave me that chance.

More than anything I want to leave this place. Demons sound like heaven, pun intended, to what faces me now. But for my family, as with all things, I will sacrifice. And a part of me hates my companions for that. So much anger wakes the beast, but now is not the time to let him loose. I have one goal; secure a nights rest for the gang. If they can give me more? Great. If not, we will find our way.

Ezekiel doesn't know me like the others and moves to wish me luck. But Rudy thankfully intercepts him. Good lucks and pep talks are verbal acknowledgement that what you're facing is no good. You don't need a pep talk if victory is eminent. And who needs good luck when the cards are in their favor? Better to say nothing at all.

Without further delay I force myself up the cobble stone path lined by lavender and Douglas Iris. The gravel between the stepping stones skitters about as I shuffle forward. My reluctance isn't one easily shaken. And though the path looks never ending, I face the wooden steps all too soon.

Another deep breath starts reconstruction on my walls and protects me enough that going up the steps does not kill me. Shaking like the ground during an earthquake I make my way to the massive doors. They dwarf me. It's almost poetic.

One last massive barrier between me and my nightmare.

I could walk away. Turn around, follow the twining path back to the truck, hop in and come up with another plan. But the others need me. And now I need these strangers behind the doors. So I grab the brass knocker before I can chicken out and bang it three times.

Those massive doors, the last barrier, swing open with ease. As they do all that brick, steel and spikes surrounding the fragile organ inside my rib cage comes crashing down. The man standing before me takes my heart firmly in his hand with nothing but a smile. He's my dad. My real dad.

The resemblance is uncanny. It's right down to the shape of my eyes-- almond. They are his, but the eye color varies. His are a warm, welcoming brown. Like a hug. Slicked back, his hair is thick and incredibly black; like my own. Even my nose, strong yet delicate, is a mirror of the man in front of me. The deadly cheek bones? My dad's too.

During all this, he's been speaking to me and finally I wonder what he must be thinking. On his doorstep stands a girl barely tall enough to reach his shoulders -- apparently I didn't receive the short gene from him -- filthy, bloody and bruised, weapons strapped to every available inch and zoned out.

I clear my throat and attempt to sound grown. "I apologize to barge in on you like this, but are you Alexander Sanctus?" My attempt fails miserably as tremors reveal me to be what I truly am; a scared child.

He hesitates and my stomach nearly drops, but then he says, "Yes, may I help you?" There's a distinct pause at the end. A blank he means for me to fill.

Here goes nothing. "I'm Leila. Your daughter."

Bomb dropped. I wait for the explosion.

The End. For now.

About the Author

Nikki Avila is on track to receive her Associates Degree for Transfer in English in 2017 from West Valley Community College.

She has plans of minoring in creative writing and majoring in American literature.

When she's not chasing after the kids she nannies or learning a new choke in jiu jitsu, she's at home writing.

Nikki lives in San Jose, CA with her big, crazy, lovable family.

www.ingramcontent.com/pod-product-compliance
Lightning Source LLC
Chambersburg PA
CBHW070647180626
46817CB00006B/2266